BOOK ONE

Fiendish Deeds

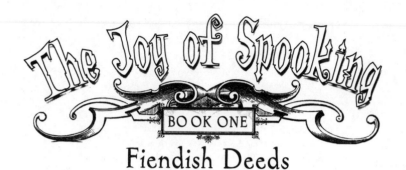

The Joy of Spooking

BOOK ONE

Fiendish Deeds

P. J. Bracegirdle

Margaret K. McElderry Books
New York   London   Toronto   Sydney

Margaret K. McElderry Books

An imprint of Simon & Schuster Children's Publishing Division

1230 Avenue of the Americas, New York, New York 10020

This book is a work of fiction. Any references to historical events, real
people, or real locales are used fictitiously. Other names, characters,
places, and incidents are products of the author's imagination, and any
resemblance to actual events or locales or persons, living or dead, is
entirely coincidental.

Book design by Debra Sfetsios

The text for this book is set in ITC Berkeley Oldstyle BT.

Manufactured in the United States of America

2 4 6 8 10 9 7 5 3 1

Library of Congress Cataloging-in-Publication Data

Bracegirdle, P. J.

Fiendish deeds / P. J. Bracegirdle.—1st ed.

p. cm.—(The joy of Spooking ; bk. #1)

Summary: As eleven-year-old Joy Wells, proud resident of the nearly
abandoned town of Spooking, tries to stop construction of a water park
in a bog she believes is home to a monster and the setting of her favorite
horror story, a man with his own mysterious connection to Spooking will
do anything to stop her.

ISBN-13: 978-1-4169-3416-5 (hardcover)

ISBN-10: 1-4169-3416-2 (hardcover)

[1. Swamps—Fiction. 2. Endangered species—Fiction. 3. Brothers and
sisters—Fiction. 4. Mystery and detective stories.] I. Title.

PZ7.B6987Joy 2008

[Fic]—dc22

2007023826

For Susan—
who first drew me with chalk

Fiendish Deeds

CHAPTER 1

From childhood's hour I have not been
As others were—I have not seen
As others saw.
~Edgar Allen Poe

Spooking—the terrible town on the hideous hill.

A crooked road leads to it from a black buzzing bog, climbing up in sharp, zigzagging turns over dizzying drops . . . to the summit, where endless headstones appear, vanishing into the distant gloom. Overgrown and askew, they lie broken against their gray neighbors—trapped in a prison of old sorrows guarded by stone walls and iron spikes.

Beyond this ancient cemetery, the cracked avenues of Spooking begin. Dark and oppressive, lined with huge overhanging maples and oaks. In their shadow, crumbling residences loom, their former glory disfigured by broken shingles and peeling paint. Drafty old mansions, standing impossibly against the onslaught of time—each sinister and terrible, they flash with menace whenever a storm rolls in.

So might have said someone from Darlington—the modern, orderly city that sprawled out around Spooking Hill. So they might have said, that is, were the citizens of

Darlington typically given to such observation, which they most certainly were not. And why should they be? They had no interest in exploring that creepy old town on the hill, living as they did in such a nice, tidy community; in happy little homes with gleaming roofs and colorful vinyl siding that never peeled. All identical and built in neat little rows, with freshly mowed lawns glittering green under the snicker-snacking of automated sprinkler systems. In Darlington there were no twisted trees, no tangled briar, no choking weeds. And no crow-infested graveyards full of crumbling old bones.

Which was exactly how the Darlings, as they were called, liked it.

But looking out from her curious round room, down at the ever-burning city lights, Joy Wells had a decidedly different view. For instance, did the Darlings ever consider how a wind howling across a drafty gable might make a roaring fire feel cozy? Or how rain pounding the tin roof above made you feel all the more snug tucked up under a thick pile of old blankets?

Joy doubted it. Darlings, in her experience, were no more given to reflection than observation.

True, Spooking was a bit rundown. The looming ornamented houses, no longer fashionable, were mostly left to fall in on themselves these days. The remainder of the town was no better, really. Once a lush landscaped arboretum, the rambling park off the Boulevard had become a neglected mess of tangled woods and cascading ponds dripping brown liquid into each other. The red brick library stood locked and lifeless, its vast collection of books gathering dust inside. The children's playground looked like the wreckage of some old bomber long shot out of the sky. Across from the playground, the high walls of Spooking Asylum blocked not only the view but even the sun most days. The asylum walls continued down toward the center of the town where a few shuttered little shops sat silent and empty.

Then there was the old cemetery, and that was about it.

But to Joy Wells, of Number 9 Ravenwood Avenue, it was everything. She closed her heavy curtains with a heavy sigh.

The house was cold as always and Joy could see her breath as she made her way down the staircase, which swept in wide ovals to the ground floor. She stopped on the landing for a moment, pressing her face to the glass of a small leaded window. Wiping away the fog, she saw with a thrill the outline of the graveyard in the distance, clearly lit under the moonlight. A stiff breeze shook the spidery trees of her street as dead leaves careened through the air and crashed back to earth.

It was a perfect Spooking night out there, all right.

The drawing room was a large round room, directly beneath Joy's bedroom. It was sparsely furnished with two wingback chairs, a small love seat, a pair of bridge lamps, and a worn old Persian rug. Joy noticed the white ash in the stone hearth with disappointment. How could she read down here without a bright roaring fire?

Mr. and Mrs. Wells sat quietly, each in their own small pools of light. Joy's little brother, Byron, lay on the floor in the shadows, engaged in high drama with a couple of action figures. Joy sat down grumpily on the love seat.

"Did you see this bill from the plumber?" Mr. Wells said suddenly, pulling at the point of his trimmed beard. "Look here—he charges *twice* my hourly rate! Unbelievable!"

"That's awful, dear," said Mrs. Wells, turning the pages of a thick book.

"It took me six years to become a lawyer. Six years! How long does it take to graduate plumbing school, I wonder?"

"I haven't a clue," said Mrs. Wells. "Except that much of the time is surely spent with one's hand down a toilet."

From the hall came a loud shuddering sound.

"And listen to that—the pipes are still banging!"

"Yes, dear." Mrs. Wells continued reading, her dark-framed glasses perched impossibly on the end of her nose, and her black hair tightly tied up in a bun. How Joy wished she had hair the same color. Instead of the unfathomable black of her mother, she was stuck with *sunny* blond, which hung perfectly straight in a cheerful honeyed sheet. It was an outrage.

Still, it suited Mrs. Wells, who was a professor in the Department of Philosophy at Wiskatempic University, a storied college standing on the banks of the north-flowing river of the same name. Like Spooking, the old campus had been swallowed up within the Municipality of Darlington. Despite the loss of its leafy grounds, the school still attracted a few students owing to a notable humanities program. Mrs. Wells specialized in existentialism, a subject she had been delighted to explain to her daughter meant the study of why one exists. The question—and the noisy pipes—had kept Joy awake many a night since.

Mr. Wells, on the other hand, was a lawyer with the firm Pennington, Plover, & Freep, a job that left him with too little time to properly match his socks, much less ponder his existence.

But even with two working professionals in their midst, the Wells family was not particularly wealthy, which was how they'd come to live in Spooking. According to Mrs. Wells, it was a frugal decision: Why would anyone buy a tiny little property in Darlington when they could buy an enormous house up in Spooking for the same price? Mr. Wells had countered that the additional expense in renovations and upkeep actually made Spooking twice as expensive in the end. However, in the ensuing debate between two towering intellects, the powers of argumentation of the philosopher proved to be superior to those of the lawyer—especially since the philosopher involved was the immovable Mrs. Wells.

And so they moved to Spooking with a young Joy and baby Byron in tow. And big it was, their new house, perfect for the epic games of hide-and-seek to come. While Joy stood counting at the hearth in the drawing room, Byron could race down the hall to the white-tiled kitchen that looked like a butcher's shop, or across to the dining room with its long table and enormous chandelier. Or flee upstairs to hide behind the high library drapes or under the overstuffed chairs in the study. Or sneak into one of the bedrooms such as Joy's, at the very top of what on the outside resembled an evil wizard's tower with its steep scaled roof. Or his parents' room, with a huge four-poster bed to slip under, and cavernous wardrobes; or his own, which, although smaller, was cluttered beyond compare, offering many secret spots to squeeze into. He could even climb up to the arched attic that was the happy home to an extended family of pigeons; or, when feeling particularly brave, head down to the cool clamminess of the cellar, crammed full of the belongings of previous owners, stacked up in moldy cardboard boxes and teetering on rickety shelves.

Then there were the guest bedrooms, the pantry, the scullery, and endless closets . . . So big was the house, that often a whole hour passed before a frustrated Joy announced loudly that she wasn't playing anymore.

Mrs. Wells often bragged that they had all the space a family could ever want, yet were only a short drive from every convenience of the city. Mr. Wells mostly grumbled that he could never find time to fix up the place and could never save up enough to hire professional contractors—especially since they all seemed to charge extra to work in Spooking.

"Aren't you going to light a fire?" Joy asked finally after her parents ignored her theatrical sighs.

Her parents looked up from their reading, startled.

"Tonight? I shouldn't think so," answered Mr. Wells. "It's warm enough in here," he explained, his words producing vaporous puffs.

"Joy, it is really time for bed," said Mrs. Wells. "And I mean straight to sleep—no reading tonight. I don't know how you can get a proper rest, sitting up with all those scary stories. They must keep you lying awake all night terrified!"

"No," said Joy defensively. But it wasn't completely true.

The Compleat and Collected Works of E. A. Peugeot had been keeping Joy awake all night—however, not from terror. In fact, she was mesmerized by the leather-bound volume. For the past month, as the downstairs clock tolled the early-morning hours, Joy delicately turned page after fragile page, poring over each word of every bizarre tale. But then her mother had caught her, when she noticed the light from Joy's bedside lamp leaking under the door to the hall.

The book had come to her by way of the Zott estate. Pennington, Plover, & Freep had given Joy's father the unenviable job of sifting through the dust-covered effects of Ms. Gertrude Zott in search of some sort of will. At over a hundred years old, Ms. Zott was Spooking's most venerable resident. Her final age was unknown, as it turned out that she had in fact died some years before being dis-covered still upright in her easy chair in a completely mum-mified state. On her lap sat an unfinished needlepoint of a duck in sunglasses drinking a cocktail at the beach.

For a week Mr. Wells endured both the lingering smell of death and the wheezing asthma brought on by the intense clouds of dust created upon disturbing any article. He then finally stumbled across the old woman's will. It said simply:

"I hereby bequeath my first edition copy of *The Compleat and Collected Works of E. A. Peugeot* to a spirited young Spooking lady with a taste for mystery, a thirst for adventure, and an eye for the inscrutable.

"The rest of it, including this house and all of my worldly possessions therein, please flatten with one of those giant balls on a chain."

Soon after, in accordance with her wishes, the building and its considerable contents were so destroyed. Mr. Wells promptly gave Joy the book—which he had recovered from under a pile of celebrity magazines in Ms. Zott's downstairs bathroom—and considered it a job ready for billing.

Joy, however, was completely bewildered. Why in the world would someone she hardly knew leave her a book? Her father's shrugging and stammering offered little in the way of explanation. But soon she had forgotten her initial suspicions, becoming utterly engrossed in the weird world living within the book's pages—a curiously familiar world. . . .

"Bedtime, Joy."

"How come Byron gets to stay up?" demanded Joy.

"Byron?" said Mrs. Wells. "Isn't he already in bed?"

"He's right there on the floor in front of you."

Mrs. Wells jumped in her seat. "Byron!" she cried, clutching her chest. "Can't you play less quietly?"

Byron scuttled away, his stocky little body slipping noiselessly under the loveseat where Joy sat.

"Both of you—kisses and then bed," said Mr. Wells absently as he pored over more bills.

The children kissed their parents and headed upstairs. Byron sprinted ahead. His oversize round head sprouted his mother's dark hair, and his little ears stuck out a bit.

Reaching the landing, he headed down the hall to his room. The ancient floor boards groaned and popped whenever anyone walked on them, but under Byron's slippered feet, they made not the slightest creak. He had a talent in that department, and it made him a formidable hide-and-seek opponent.

Joy's room was dimly lit blue by the aquarium. As she entered, a large green bullfrog inside suddenly sat up on its hind legs and made a loud sound. Not quite like a dog, but not quite like a frog, either.

"No, Fizz, you've had enough food for today."

Fizz barked again.

"Bad frog!" scolded Joy. "Lie down!"

Fizz ran clumsily in circles, now yelping loudly.

"Oh, all right then!" Joy tossed him a crunchy dog treat in the shape of a bone. "You'll have to eat it in the dark, though," she said, switching off his lamp. *Just as well,* she thought. Fizz slobbering over a treat until it was soft enough to swallow was not something she wanted to watch. Why couldn't he just eat creepy-crawlies like every other frog?

Joy headed to the bathroom. She brushed her teeth vigorously, watching her mouth froth over in the bathroom mirror. Just like some creature, she thought, insane with hunger for human flesh. She gargled and spat, frowning at herself. Well, she didn't have a particularly mysterious hair color, but she had to admit to feeling somewhat satisfied with her eyes, which shone an eerie gray with tiny flecks of gold.

Back in her room, she quickly put on her pajamas and

jumped under icy sheets. With the bedside light on and *The Compleat and Collected Works* propped up with her knees, she read for the thousandth time the graceful inscription in sepia ink:

"To my beloved—A."

She closed the book, reached for a postmarked envelope on her bedside table, and dumped its contents on the blanket. Flushing with pride, she read again:

Dear <u>Miss Joy Wells</u>,

We would like to officially confirm receipt of your money order, and welcome you as a member of the Ethan Alvin Peugeot Society.

Please find enclosed ~~our quarterly newsletter~~, a biography of Mr. Peugeot prepared by the Society, ~~and a limited edition EAP Society mouse pad~~.

Regards,

Richard Strang

President and Treasurer, EAP Society

At the bottom, written with a leaky pen:

Mouse pad on back-order—sorry!

The biography was a booklet made of folded photocopies stapled crookedly together. What it lacked in production values, it made up for in content, Joy thought. She flipped again to the picture of Peugeot—one of the few that existed, so it said underneath. He sat bent forward in a stuffed chair, posing awkwardly, his hands clasped together on his lap, looking somehow like a bird on an unsteady perch. He wore a dark buttoned-up suit with a tightly knotted scarf and downcast mustache, his oiled black hair curled at the front and parted severely at the side.

He was handsome, Joy decided. Well, sort of. She stared at his sharp features, thrown into dramatic shadow by some unseen lamp. With an uneasy expression, Peugeot stared back—imparting an eerie feeling that he was actually gazing right out of the photograph itself. His dark eyes seemed to look ever so slightly over her shoulder, at something lurking behind her. It gave her the creeps, a feeling that was most welcome.

"Put the light out now," said the disembodied head of Mrs. Wells in the bedroom doorway, causing Joy to throw down the booklet in fright. "I don't want to hear the bus honking for you tomorrow because you've overslept again."

"Okay, okay," answered Joy, switching off the lamp. "Good night, Mom."

"Good night, dear."

The door clunked shut.

Joy lay in the blackness, listening to the floor boards groan as her mother tramped down the hall. The toilet flushed. She heard her mother talking softly, her father's wheezy cough. Then it was silent again. Except for the wind, that is, and the sound of something scraping against the side of the house.

A branch perhaps? Or something else. *Something* that wanted in. . . .

She threw off the blankets and crept to the window to peer into the night. It was now stormy outside, the lights of Darlington vanished behind a boiling mist. She scanned the inky darkness along the side of the house—then spotted the source of the ceaseless scraping. It *was* only a tree, she confirmed. Oh well.

Tiptoeing across the chilly floor, Joy kicked the rug up against the bottom of the door, then quickly jumped back in bed. She put the light back on and opened the book where the length of red ribbon marked the page she had left off.

"The Terrible Town on the Hideous Hill."

Her favorite story. How much the town reminded her of Spooking!

And whether it was due to the foreknowledge of the horror to come or just her icy feet, Joy shivered deliciously.

CHAPTER 2

Seen through the heavy rain pouring across the windshield, the old shop swayed back and forth as if alive. As if in anguish, bewailing its abandoned state, pleading for someone—anyone—to flick on the lights and fire up its boiler, to begin the dirty chore of wiping away a decade of grime from its front window.

The rivulets of rain parted and the shop's pitted sign became momentarily distinct:

LUTHIER LORENZO

Beneath that, another sign:

FOR SALE

The man at the wheel stared, face blank, as memories played to the sound of the idling engine. He saw himself standing on the step in rubber boots, a shovel over his shoulder, grinning as he inhaled the sweet scents of autumnal decay. He heard the sound of his father gently hammering a fret in place with a mallet. Above he saw his mother, a ghost in the window, waving him off to work.

Then the vision disappeared, and all that remained was the filthy, dilapidated shop. He clenched his teeth. How he now hated the place and its cramped little second-floor apartment. It needed to be put out of its misery.

The car growled impatiently—a low, throaty noise befitting the huge engine that surely lurked under such an enormous hood. The man put the black car into drive and made a U-turn. The thick tires hissed on the slick road and the chromed grill shone like a bared set of teeth. He headed a short way back the way he had come, pulling onto the muddy patch in front of the cemetery gates.

The car stopped growling. The man got out, sheltered from the rain under a wide black umbrella. The galoshes protecting his shiny shoes sank in the mud as he entered.

This time, he needed no fleeting visions of yesteryear. Everything was just as it always was, the same old ghosts rising up almost visibly from their graves. In their familiar company he recalled all the wasted hours, blistering his hands and breaking his back within these long stone walls. Tending and fussing over the horror of a place like it was some sort of royal garden. Living without ambition, up to his waist in muck and digging himself in deeper. How foolish he'd been.

But no longer, he told himself. Today he strode the avenues of the dead in a suit and tie.

He recalled his conversation with the grave-digger down in Darlington—a kid really, with a pierced eyebrow, busy scooping enormous clods of earth with a backhoe. He gave the grave-digger a good story, that he was a nephew wanting to pay his respects to his beloved Uncle Ludwig, except his crazy old aunt wouldn't tell him where her husband was buried. Any chance he knew where to find him?

"Yeah, but the dude—your uncle, I mean—went in up the hill in that creepy old graveyard," he had answered. "Man, I even had to dig the hole with a shovel 'cuz I couldn't get this stupid thing in," he added, slapping a hand loudly against the frame of the backhoe. "Anyway, he's buried pretty much right in the middle, by some big stone angel swinging a sword. You can't miss it, dude," the grave-digger said finally, before popping his blaring head-phones back on.

"Thanks, *dude*," the man said, smirking as the backhoe roared to life.

Now, standing in the graveyard, he looked up at the statue—the Avenging Angel—drenched and dark, its cheeks streaming with tears as it wound up to smite him with its heavy sword.

The man looked away. To the left, he spotted a small polished granite stone standing out of place among the ancient markers. There it was, the name he sought, chiseled simply.

LUDWIG ZWEIG

He wrote it carefully in a little leather notebook, the streaming umbrella resting unsteadily on his head.

CHERISHED HUSBAND, it said underneath.

The old woman, he remembered.

He felt a flash of anger. He had had enough of this game playing. Well, one down, he thought, one to go. He turned to leave.

Another headstone caught his attention.

VERONIQUE PHIPPS

Here she was, finally, alone for eternity. He gasped.

"Your father," she'd cried down the phone. "He's gone, Octavio, and this time it's for good!"

He stood there, watching raindrops bounce off the headstone, ashamed of himself. A failure, that's what he was, a failure of a son. He couldn't have saved her from being alone in the grave, but maybe he could have made her a little less lonely at the end of her poor life.

His father, however, no one could have saved. Not from his cursed blood.

The same blood that coursed through his own veins, he knew. At the thought, he felt a tingling feeling in his fingertips. He raised one hand in front of his face and stared hard. It looked solid enough, he thought. Probably just numbness from gripping the umbrella too tightly.

But he had to get out of there—the place wasn't good for his nerves. He weaved without sympathy through the gray markers of other long-lost loved ones until he arrived back at the cemetery gates.

The black car started up angrily and then spun out toward the road. There was a sudden blast of a horn, terrifyingly close. The tires screeched as he hit the brakes.

His head slammed against the steering wheel, hard enough to honk back at the bright yellow blur roaring by. It was a school bus, full of children, their round faces pressed up against the windows above him. He swore, rubbing the swelling egg above his eyebrow, as the bus careened down toward Darlington.

How he hated this hill, he raged to himself as he drove off.

❧ ❧ ❧

Every day, the children of Spooking rode the bus past the cemetery, down the hill to school in Darlington. And every day, they received the same rousing welcome.

"THE GHOULS ON THE BUS GO ROUND AND ROUND, ROUND AND ROUND, ROUND AND ROUND. THE GHOULS ON THE BUS GO ROUND AND ROUND, ALL OVER TOWN!"

It was a tradition Joy had endured since her first day at Winsome Elementary. Six years later, it showed no signs of abating. With an evil hiss the bus would come to a stop, pitching the kids of Spooking forward in their seats as pudgy fists pounded the windows and fat faces bobbed up screaming. The door would then fold open violently.

"OFF!"

Burdened by school bags and lunch boxes, the Spookys would then march straight through the wall of taunts and abuse into school. There, hopelessly outnumbered, they did their best not to draw any more attention to themselves than necessary.

And so it had gone that morning as Joy sat down at her desk—an old wooden one, carved and chipped over countless semesters, with a little round hole at the top right where a bottle of ink used to go. A desk that was riddled with secrets, Joy decided, as she spent long afternoons deciphering the puzzle of scribbles on its surface. For instance, did Edith really love Ezra? Or was it just some cruel torment? Perhaps the answer lay in that illegible blob of smudged marker. . . .

The others' desks in the class were new, each with steel legs and a Formica top that had an almost supernatural ability to destroy the tip of any pen foolish enough to mark on it. Exactly how her old desk had ended up there among them was a mystery. But she was fond of it, even grateful that it had been forced on her the first day of school by the sharp elbows of the other children.

Joy yawned—the teacher was late. She looked up at the familiar poster of an old, crazy-haired man with his tongue sticking out. "Imagination is more important than knowledge," it said underneath. The man was Albert Einstein, Joy knew, the big genius, who even Mrs. Wells reluctantly acknowledged was smarter than your average logical positivist.

The teacher came in, laying her coat on her desk. "Sorry I'm late! Children, how *are* we today?"

"GREAT, MISS KEENER!" answered the class in a single exuberant voice.

Except for Joy, that is, who pretended to cough, like she did every morning. Coughed, or sneezed, or fetched a pencil that just happened to roll onto the floor. . . .

"Terrific! Is everyone excited to continue with the book reports today?"

"YEAH!" shouted the class.

"Wow! You sound like you all had a great breakfast!" she remarked, laughing.

Miss Keener had a thing about breakfasts. If you didn't eat a proper one, not only were you unable to concentrate in class but you were also much more likely to end up in prison later, possibly on death row. An unbalanced lunch, meanwhile, foreshadowed not only brittle-bone syndrome but a career in the toilet-cleaning trade, Joy had been informed.

"Okay, let me pull a name. . . ." Miss Keener picked up a large top hat and stirred the contents. "I do hope Mr. Fluffs didn't get in and eat any of them!"

Mr. Fluffs was the class rabbit. Using the hat, Miss Keener was able to make him vanish into thin air. It was a good trick but hardly the equal of Mr. Fluffs's own magic act, wherein he disappeared into the shredded newspaper of his cage for an entire week before reappearing with yet another disgusting eye infection.

"Abracadabra! Abracadoo! Who's going next? Who is it? Who?"

Please don't pick my name, thought Joy. *Please.*

Joy knew such a pathetic attempt to alter the course of fate was pointless—her name was in there somewhere, and Miss Keener wouldn't stop fishing for it until the hat was empty of everything save a few crusty flakes from Mr. Fluff's eye. But she couldn't help herself.

Miss Keener read from a small piece of paper. "Tyler!" A couple of chimpanzee-like whoops came from the back of class.

"I'm ready, Miss," said Tyler, swaggering up to the blackboard, where he cleared his throat theatrically. "For this report, I decided to choose a really famous story that most everybody knows."

"Great," purred Miss Keener. "Let's hear about it."

"It's based on the TV show *Ultradroids*." Upon hearing

the title, a few boys started humming something that Joy guessed was the *Ultradroids* theme song. "*Take out the trash, Ultradroid captains!*" yelled Tyler, striking an action pose. The class erupted into laughter.

"Now settle down, everyone," said Miss Keener mildly. "Okay, *Ultradroids*—cool," she said, snapping her fingers and bobbing her head to show she was down with it. Joy cringed. "Go on, Tyler."

"Yeah, so it's a wicked show as everybody who lives on this planet knows. And this is the book version." Tyler held a copy up. The cover featured a gigantic robot bristling with missiles in a similar pose to the one Tyler had struck moments before. "Well, actually, there's like twenty-eight books or something. But this one is Number 7: *The Destruction of Homeworld.*"

Tyler looked at his sheet. "There's no author listed, so I left that part blank. What's next? Oh yeah, the story.

"So the Ultradroids are returning from fighting the Legion of the Overlord again, but instead of their home planet, they see this cloud of broken-up rocks. . . ."

Tyler began outlining the major plot points. They involved his crawling around on all fours while firing barrage after barrage of imaginary missiles from his hands, feet, back, and even his eyes in one dramatic instance. The resulting explosions left a fine mist of saliva swirling in front of the class, making Joy once again thankful that she sat near the back.

"So their planet wasn't really destroyed," Tyler concluded, wiping his chin. "It was all a dream Commander Slate had when he was unconscious after his Ultradroid was hit by a pulse rocket." He let loose a final, incredible explosion of spittle. "But everything was actually okay the whole time! So if you read it yourself, don't worry, because everything works out in the end. Thank you."

There was loud applause as Tyler took a bow. Joy marveled at how Tyler's spoiling the ending made *The Destruction of Homeworld* an even less likely read.

"Thank you, Tyler," said Miss Keener. "I can see you really enjoyed reading that book! Wouldn't you say that *reading* about Ultradroids was a better experience than just *watching* Ultradroids on television?"

Tyler shrugged. "Not really, Miss Keener. It took me a week to read the book, but I can watch a whole episode in just a half hour. Television is a much more *efficient* way to enjoy Ultradroids, I think."

"Well, that's certainly a valid point, Tyler," said Miss Keener. "Thank you—you may take your seat. Now allakazam, allakazoo. Who's going next, who, who?" Miss Keener drew another name. "Cassandra!"

Joy decided to tune out Cassandra's book report, which not surprisingly involved a pale young lady with a secret, a troublesome pony, and a handsome farmhand. She began thinking about last night, and how she'd woken to more scratching sounds outside. This time, however, there was no wind and she could see from her bed that the trees weren't moving. So she'd crept to the window to scan the shadows of the front lawn—just in time to get a glimpse of something bolting away.

Unfortunately, in the morning she discovered that a particularly deep sleep had left her memory a bit fuzzy, and she was now unsure exactly what she'd seen. So, as Cassandra droned on in the background, Joy began clearing her mind of all thoughts until the image became clear again. The results she excitedly sketched in the margin of her notebook.

But it just didn't look right. Somehow it looked less like some monster and more like an overweight cat.

"Joy," said Miss Keener.

Joy dropped her pencil. She looked up, startled, and saw Miss Keener with the magic hat on her lap, holding up a slip of paper.

"Are you ready to do your book report, Joy?" asked Miss Keener.

Joy nodded. *Just get it over with,* she thought. She quickly collected her folder of papers and rushed up to the blackboard.

"For my report," she began, trembling slightly as she addressed the class, "I chose a story called 'The Bawl of the Bog Fiend.'"

There were a couple of snickers.

"That's 'bawl,' with a *w*—it's another word for 'cry,'" she explained. "Anyway, the story was written by Ethan Alvin Peugeot, who lived over a hundred years ago. E. A. Peugeot wrote many stories, poems, and essays, and is considered one of the greatest contributors to suspense and horror literature of all time. 'The Bawl of the Bog Fiend' is the first story where we meet Peugeot's best-known character, paranormal investigator Dr. Lyndon Ingram."

Joy opened the stapled booklet from the EAP Society, which now had several paragraphs delicately underlined in pencil.

"Interestingly, Mr. Peugeot is believed to have lived somewhere in this area—near Darlington," she added spontaneously, "although of course it didn't exist back then. Exactly where he lived has always been a cause for much speculation," she said, referring to the EAP Society biography.

"You see, Mr. Peugeot was a very mysterious person. He lived under false names and wore disguises. And there were all sorts of crazy rumors about him." Joy read out: "'There are even people to this day who believe that his supernatural stories were in some or all part true accounts of his extraordinary life.'

"He ultimately vanished from the face of the earth, never to be seen again."

Joy glanced up. The class was listening intently.

"This is perhaps the greatest mystery of all," she continued, "As the story goes, Mr. Peugeot only appeared at his publisher's offices once a year, around October, when he would drop off new manuscripts and get paid before disappearing again.

"Then one year he did not show up. The publisher finally hired a private detective to go look for him. A month later, the detective sent a telegram to the publisher's office.

"It said: FOUND OUT WHAT HAPPENED TO EAP STOP GETTING TRAIN BACK TONIGHT STOP," she read out dramatically. "But the detective never returned—he, too, vanished without a trace.

"The only clue was this final telegram. But no one was

even sure where it was sent from, as the receiving office noted it with only four letters: SPKG."

"SPKG?" repeated Miss Keener.

"It was shorthand," explained Joy. "For the place where the telegram was sent."

The class was dead silent.

"Well?" asked Miss Keener. "Did anyone ever figure it out?"

"No," replied Joy. "I mean, not until I did." Her voice rose in triumph. "It was short for *Spooking!*"

CHAPTER 3

After lunch an announcement came over the PA system, summoning the children to the auditorium. Principal Crawley stood at the podium onstage, signaling the students to take their seats in an orderly fashion. He wore a sweater in a tangerine and teal diamond pattern under his ever-present corduroy jacket, the knot of his tie painfully cinched as if he had just climbed down from an unsuccessful attempt to hang himself.

The loudspeakers suddenly squealed horribly.

"Whoa," said Mr. Crawley, adjusting the microphone. "That was certainly an ear SPLITTER . . . WHOA, VOLUME! VOLUME! TESTING, testing, testing, one, two, three. That's better.

"Ahem, good afternoon, children. I've called an assembly because we have a special guest here today. Please give a big Winsome welcome to Darlington's own Mayor Mungo MacBrayne!"

There was an explosion of applause from the dutiful children as the red velvet curtains rippled to life. Clapping and whooping with increasing enthusiasm, they watched as the curtains began boiling like the surface of a stormy sea. Then finally, just as the children began examining their stinging hands and clutching their aching throats, a man emerged, stumbling onto the stage.

He was an impressive figure, powerfully plump, like some mythological wrestler who had forsaken his toga for a tan suit. His hair was golden and ridiculously plentiful, with the tight curls of a cherub. In an incredible display, he instantly replaced an expression of absolute disgust with a broad blinding smile. His balance and dignity restored, the mayor crossed over to Principal Crawley and proceeded to crush his hand into paste.

At that moment, Joy glimpsed a pale man in a dark suit struggling with the curtains, looking flustered, embarrassed, and angry all at once.

Much like she'd probably looked earlier, Joy imagined, as the class laughed at her theory about the detective's disappearance. Why had she bothered telling a bunch of brain-dead Darlings anyway? They'd never believe that someone as important and famous as Ethan Alvin Peugeot had ever lived in Spooking, or that the detective tailing him had vanished there. It wasn't worth even arguing with them. Joy had instead stammered her way through her report before Tyler's snickering at her use of the word "bawl" set the whole class off again, at which point Miss Keener told her to take a seat.

Joy watched the man, now flailing at the curtains murderously. With a final violent yank, he vanished from view.

"Thank you, Principal Crawley," said Mayor MacBrayne, taking the podium. "You may not know this, but once upon a time, Principal Crawley and I were both students here at Winsome, back when the school first opened." The children looked dumbly at Principal Crawley, who nodded in agreement. "And if I recall correctly, Peter, we were both in Mrs. Windlesworth's grade six class together."

Principal Crawley laughed and shook his head, offering a correction that was not picked up by the microphone.

"Well, her name started with a *W*, so close enough," continued Mayor MacBrayne irritably. "The point is, what different paths we took from that same class, all those years ago. You see, the journey of life is a wondrous thing. There are no maps, and no rest stops. You follow the signs as best you can, and suddenly you're there. Wherever you are, that is.

"Myself, I went on to become a leading industrialist—which means a really rich businessman, kids," he explained with a wink, "before recently being elected mayor of Darlington in the greatest landslide victory ever recorded in the city's history.

"Principal Crawley, on the other hand, stayed right here at Winsome. Which is also great! Because where would we be in life if some people didn't stay right where they are, helping others to get off to a great start? Give him a hand, folks!"

The children obliged, but quickly discovered their hands were still smarting from the sustained applause earlier, managing only a small pitter-patter of appreciation.

"Anyway, I'm not here today to reminisce about the past—I am here to look to the future! And by that, I mean the results of the Darlington, City of the Future competition!"

There were cheers.

"Now, the day after I was elected, I sat down at City Hall and asked my colleagues a question: How can we make Darlington even better? How can we not only keep Darlington a great place to live, but make it somewhere that everyone across the country wants to visit? In short, how are we going to make Darlington *really cool*?

"Well, they didn't have any answers. They're great people, my colleagues—great, great people—but they just didn't know. Meaning no disrespect, their ideas were old and tired, frankly.

"So I said to myself: Who *would* know? Who *are* the future of Darlington anyway? And then it struck me—the children. So I came up with the idea of having your teachers get you each to write an essay about what *you* wanted to see in Darlington's future. We wanted your highest hopes. Your biggest dreams! And to make it even more exciting, we offered a prize for the winning entry.

"And oh boy, did we get some amazing ideas!" The mayor pointed into the audience, shouting: "A giant shopping plaza in the shape of a flying saucer! A towering complex of toy boutiques in the shape of an Ultradroid! And a mile-high megamall even more mega than the Darlington Megamall! All great, great ideas," he finished. "But one of you really stepped up to the plate with a truly exciting plan. Something that could put Darlington on the map, and not just as a great place for shopping. Something to make it one of the most exciting places on the whole seaboard.

"The young lad with the big plan . . . A drum roll,

please . . . is Morris Mealey! Come on up here, son!"

"YES, YES, YES!" A boy leaped out of his seat and sprinted down the aisle to the stage, taking the stairs two at a time. He skidded to a stop in front of the mayor and began pumping his fist in the air in victory. MacBrayne clapped a huge hand onto one of his slim shoulders to calm him.

"So how does it feel, Morris Mealey, to be a winner?" the mayor asked.

"It's Morris M. Mealey," corrected the boy loudly into the microphone.

"That's great, son," replied Mayor MacBrayne. "Mr. Phipps!" he called offstage. "Unveil Stage One!"

As the pale man behind the curtains came into view again, Joy was awestruck by his fearsome appearance: his tight-fitting suit and shiny shoes, pointed like dangerous weapons; his heavy arched brow, split at one edge by a long white scar; his hair an unruly coif, tar black with a shimmering hint of blue.

In front of him he pushed a squeaky trolley on which something sat upright, covered by a sheet. He turned to the audience as he walked, gazing out at them with piercing eyes. In the center of his forehead, a swollen ugly bruise seemed to almost visibly throb.

"Behold!" cried Mayor MacBrayne, yanking the sheet away with a flourish. "The artist's conception of the new MISTY MERMAID WATER PARK! Coming soon to DARLINGTON, CITY OF THE FUTURE!"

❦ ❦ ❦

Byron Wells hadn't been paying the slightest attention to what was going on up on the stage.

How could he, when sitting directly in front of him was Lucy Primrose?

Which meant that—completely unobserved and without arousing any suspicion—he was able to bask in the golden light of her being, or at least the smaller but no less wonderful glow coming from the right side of her face as she turned to whisper to her best friend, Ella. In a semiswoon, he'd noticed the green plastic clips Lucy wore to hold back her long hair, her little ear like a cream-colored seashell below.

The fascination was quite unexpected for eight-year-old Byron. Was he the only boy this age who felt like this? He looked at the others in his row—scrawling on the backs of seats with markers, examining trading cards with a tiny camouflage flashlight, huddling over a handheld video game—and thought, *maybe it is just me.*

At any rate, such feelings were something to be kept to himself. Lucy was a Darling, after all, and he was a Spooky. Such a romantic liaison was completely unprecedented—not to mention unthinkable.

And then there was Joy. The idea of her little brother having a crush on one of those "prissy little snobs" would surely make her physically ill, at the very least. Would she ever even speak to him again?

No, it was a secret he'd resolved to take to the grave.

When he heard a loud gasp around him, Byron looked up at the stage. He was astonished to see how many people had joined Principal Crawley up there: a large bear of a man with golden hair, a spidery man in a dark suit, and someone Byron recognized as the annoying dark-haired boy from his class named Morris. Between them was a large panel depicting a system of winding slides and what appeared to be a gigantic wave rising up out of a pool. At the top it read MISTY MERMAID WATER PARK—ARTIST'S CONCEPTION.

Everyone was very excited now, including Lucy, apparently. Was it a field trip, Byron wondered? He suddenly felt scared—he didn't even know how to swim, and some of the slides looking terrifyingly high, clinging to a cliff's face.

"Once again, young Mr. Mealey, the City of Darlington appreciates your great, great idea," said the big man. "And in thanks, I am happy to offer you a season pass!" he added, handing Morris a ticket.

The children managed a burst of exhausted applause as Morris held his prize aloft, as if it were the decapitated head of a bitter enemy.

"See you all there next summer!" cried the mayor. The man in the dark suit wheeled away the display. Principal Crawley, looking at his watch worriedly, quickly dismissed everyone, and the whole auditorium descended into chaos.

The children rushed down the aisles, talking excitedly. Joy stayed in her seat, waiting for the crowd to disperse while Byron was swept out of the auditorium like a stick in a raging river. Once outside, he broke from the current and slipped into the washroom.

The boys' room was eerily quiet. Byron decided to forgo the urinals and lock himself into a stall. It was always a good precaution for a small Spooky whenever within kicking and screaming distance from things that flush.

Nevertheless, his blood froze when he heard footsteps. Hard-soled shoes. He breathed out in relief upon hearing grown-up voices.

"The boys' washroom, delightful," said a man, sounding fatigued. "I see they are still decorating the ceiling with balls of wet toilet paper."

"Don't be such a snob, Phipps," replied a man with a loud, booming voice. "When a man needs to go, he needs to go. Did you see that? How crazy the kids went? This idea is a serious moneymaker."

"Yes, Mayor. And all it cost us was a season pass to what is effectively a swamp at this point."

"You're a genius, Phipps, a real credit to the MacBrayne administration. I won't forget this, come next salary review."

"Speaking of which, when might such a review occur, sir?"

"Pure genius!" continued the man with the booming voice. "Speaking of the bog, how are the bulldozers doing? What's the current schedule for clearing it all away?"

"The bulldozers have already cleared the scrub for the parking lot, but unfortunately we can't give them the go-ahead to start major excavation and drainage until the resident vacates."

"That crazy old woman's still living in there?" The voice was alarmed. "But we need to start breaking ground! We won't get a penny more out of our investors unless they're sure we can open by next summer."

"I know, sir." There was a loud blowing of a nose. "However, the bog's a pretty lonely place for an insane old widow. Plus, I didn't mention—I was able to get the old man's full name off his gravestone this morning. Now we can easily look into their ridiculous claim. Don't worry—the project will go ahead as scheduled."

Byron could hear the tap running and the *thwump-thwump* as bubblegum-scented soap was dispensed, then the tearing of scratchy brown paper towel.

"Okay," said the man with the booming voice. "I trust you, Mr. Phipps," he said, sighing heavily.

"Thank you, sir."

There were footsteps again, then silence. Byron waited, then poked his head out. The washroom was empty.

He scurried off to class.

❧ ❧ ❧

Byron and Joy sat side by side on the bus ride home.

"What do you mean, what was that all about?" asked Joy. "Weren't you paying attention at assembly?"

"Umm, no," answered Byron stiffly, "I was . . . drawing." Byron didn't often lie to Joy, and his throat clenched like he'd inhaled the eraser off a pencil.

"The mayor said they're going to build some giant water park here," explained Joy wearily. "The Misty Mermaid or something." Joy rolled her eyes. "Mermaids, how lame is that? Why not sea monsters, or a ghost ship theme with skeleton pirates? I am sure it's going to be all disgusting and cute. . . ."

Joy then wondered what the judges had thought of her

own entry in the Darlington, City of the Future competition. It was a drawing of Byron's—the view from the ground as a hovering UFO unleashed a devastating heat ray on a happy little town. Under it she had written in large block letters: THE FUTURE?

"That big wave looked pretty scary to me," said Byron.

"That was just the artist's conception," replied Joy. "A wave like that would put the food court in the parking lot—and believe me, that's the last thing they'd want."

"What's an artist's contraption?"

"An artist's *conception*—a painting of how it might look when it's done. But it's completely imaginary, and doesn't mean a thing. I doubt very much it will actually include monorail service or somewhere to park your flying car, for example.

"What I want to know is where are they going to put it. Because if I have to wake up every morning looking out over some pathetic theme park for prissy little princesses, I am gonna puke."

Byron didn't bother speculating, but instead began staring out the window, lost in a dream. He was like that a lot lately, Joy noticed, like a sleepwalker dressed in a pair of brown corduroy pajama bottoms.

Joy, on the other hand, felt like she was in her usual waking nightmare, culminating with Miss Keener making her stay after class—for a *word*.

"You do bring these things on yourself, Joy," Miss Keener had lectured her. "I had only asked for a simple book report. And although I do appreciate that you enjoy doing extra research, in future just stick to the story, please. This isn't the first time you've taken up class time with your overactive imagination, you know."

Joy had stood staring blankly over Miss Keener's shoulder to avoid her enormous unblinking eyes, when the poster on the wall behind her came into sharp focus.

"But I thought imagination was more important than knowledge," Joy had suddenly protested, looking up at the crazy-haired man sticking his tongue out at her.

Miss Keener had just sighed wearily. "I'm afraid you have that backward, dear. Now go on, or you'll miss your bus."

Joy had slunk out without another word.

Although tempting, she'd decided not to point out that Miss Keener was no Einstein.

CHAPTER 4

The sky was an ominous flint-gray that Saturday morning as the siblings left their house.

Joy wore a tweed suit with matching coat belted tight at the waist, and a purple turtleneck. A wide-brimmed brown felt hat with a leather cord pulled tight under her chin and a pair of oxblood leather boots completed her look.

She called it her adventuring ensemble.

"Don't you feel that running around in a dead person's clothes is a bit odd for a girl of almost twelve?" Joy had once overheard her mother ask her father. From her position on the landing, she couldn't make out the muffled reply. "No, I'm not saying it's your fault, sweetness," her mother answered, "but yes, it's true that if you'd cleared out the basement as promised, she would've never gotten into all of those creepy old things. . . ."

Joy had snuck back upstairs, fuming. What business was it of theirs anyway? But she wasn't particularly worried—the likelihood of her father clearing out the basement was about as great as his building a zeppelin port on the roof.

Nevertheless, the mere thought gave her a shiver. It was one of Joy's greatest delights, raking through the dusty boxes down there. The forgotten possessions and mysterious artifacts—it was like exhuming the dead without all the noxious gas and maggots! Rifling through them, the strange old objects seemed to hum with some sort of quiet energy transmuted by their long-lost owners—as if waiting to be seized up and put to purpose again.

Joy was only too happy to oblige.

PROPERTY OF MS. MELODY HUXLEY, said the yellowed label on the trunk where Joy had found the suit, coat, and boots. Inside she'd uncovered more clothes and curios, as well a locked diary that she'd tried for hours to pick unsuccessfully. And while she supposed she could have sawn through the leather clasp, somehow it just didn't feel right to open it without a suitable display of finesse.

In addition, there were four albums thick with photos of the house's former owner, a petite woman whom Joy found beautiful with her fine features, boyish hair, and crooked smile. She was often pictured in the very same tweed suit Joy now wore. So otherworldly and cool was Ms. Huxley that Joy even forgave her apparently insatiable lust for blood, as demonstrated by her posing in photo after photo grinning with a shotgun above piles of dead birds, winking in a pith helmet among slaughtered predators, and giving the thumbs-up in front of a black roadster as she lashed a deer with a lolling tongue to the hood. It was also a different age, Joy reminded herself—one before the advent of plastic wrap and Styrofoam and the practice of packaging everything up into less distasteful portions.

So, her disconcerting penchant for blowing away all creatures feathered and furry aside, Joy saw an inspiring woman in Ms. Huxley's fading likenesses—a woman full of conviction and confidence, whether firing an arrow or hoisting a cocktail, eyes ever twinkling with mischievousness. A woman to whom life was not simply about fulfilling the expectations of others, but about defining oneself without fear or compromise.

Unfortunately, her once luxurious suit and coat now gave off a serious whiff of mold and mothballs, only slightly masked by the fragrant hat of another owner, which Joy had recovered from a nearby cedar chest. She'd looked a bit ridiculous in the sequined cloche she pulled from Ms. Huxley's trunk, after all, and doubted she could have gotten away with Ms. Huxley's pith helmet, which was a bit too tight anyway. The felt hat was a bit too big, not to mention meant for a man, but it looked like serious business with its crocodile-skin band.

Byron, on the other hand, wore his usual fall outfit: a navy peacoat over a gray cable sweater, with brown corduroys that instead of pooling around his ankles were today stuffed uncomfortably into a pair of rubber boots, which were full of crumbs of dried mud.

As they reached the end of the path, a knobby green head poked out from a leather shoulder bag at Joy's side. With school in session, Fizz was spending a lot more time in his aquarium—Joy thought he could use some fresh Spooking air. "No, Fizz, it's too far to hop," she told him, stroking his smooth, clammy throat. "You can go on your leash when we reach the bog."

"The bog?" asked Byron in surprise, not expecting such an epic hike. "What for?"

"I'm looking for mushrooms. Giant ones, specifically of the deadly poisonous variety."

"How come?"

"Monday is Teacher Appreciation Day, and I was thinking of making a nice quiche for Miss Keener."

Byron went white.

"It was just a joke, sheesh." Joy laughed, looking at his face. "No, last night I was reading over an E. A. Peugeot story, 'The Bawl of the Bog Fiend'—"

"It's not the story with the glass slippers and the pumpkin, is it?"

"Not 'ball,' Byron. And that isn't a Peugeot story—it's Cinderella!" Joy shivered with disgust. "I said 'bawl,' with a *w*—it's an old-fashioned word for 'cry.' Now I forgot what I was saying!"

"Sorry."

"Oh yeah, so I was reading it again and noticed a very interesting detail I'd missed. In this story, Dr. Ingram is investigating a rash of gruesome killings around a bog near the town. It all starts when a rich local begins trying to drain the bog so he can build a pig farm there, because apparently even back then, you could never have enough bacon. But then, one of his workers disturbs something ancient and incredibly grouchy."

"What?" asked Byron as they reached the end of Ravenwood

Avenue and turned onto Spooking Boulevard.

"I'll get to that. The point is that when Dr. Ingram and his assistant venture in—Dickson is his assistant's name this time—they soon come across something. 'A *ring of striking specimens, hooded and monstrous, resembling in all but size a genus deadly to anything seeking the source of its sweet scent.'* Or something like that.

"Anyway, just as they are going in for a closer look, Dickson falls down a hole and gets one of those really gross broken legs where the bone sticks out. Dr. Ingram begs him to be quiet, as the creature, he says, is attracted to sounds of distress! But it was no use! Because Dickson had in fact fallen right into *the fetid den of the bog fiend!*"

"He fell into what?"

"The fetid den of the bog fiend."

Byron looked at her blankly.

"The creature's stinky lair, basically," she said.

"What the heck is a bog fiend anyway?"

As they passed the towering homes of Weredale Avenue and Gravesend Lane, Joy explained how the bog fiend was a horrible-smelling creature with hooked claws, long tusks, and a mouthful of razor-sharp teeth. Other than that, its exact appearance had never been credibly established owing to its incredible speed. Peugeot described the creature as large enough to snatch a horse from a passing carriage, and ill-mannered enough to vomit bloody entrails in the exact spot where a fleeing Dr. Ingram would later trip and face-plant. Further details were sketchy at best.

"Okay, so another horrible monster," said Byron, showing

less amazement than Joy felt the retelling deserved. "But what do mushrooms have to do with it?"

"Hello, are you even listening? What did Dr. Ingram just stumble across before finding the lair of the bog fiend? Something hooded and edible that lives in a bog! Which means mushrooms, of course. Except these babies are huge and poisonous."

Byron made a face. "But you said they smelled sweet, which mushrooms don't."

"They do too, if you sauté them!" snapped Joy. "Don't get all picky on my theory. The point is, if we just look for the same giant poisonous mushrooms, we'll have a good shot at locating the entrance of *the fetid den of the*—"

"Whoa, wait a sec," interrupted Byron. "Are you telling me you really think there are such things as bog fiends?"

Which was a fair question.

Joy had encountered similar doubt from her mother one morning after Joy had again heard something big shuffling across the yard in the night. She had raced to the window and this time caught sight of something crashing through the hedges, heading toward the cemetery.

"It was probably just a raccoon," Mrs. Wells had said dismissively.

"No way, it was bigger," Joy had replied. "Plus it had a shiny black back, like it was covered in leathery skin or something."

Mr. Wells had put down his newspaper. "Now, if a creature like that was running around Spooking, don't you think we'd already have proof?" he pointed out.

Proof. Her father always insisted on it. In order to be true, something must always be proved, he held. Otherwise, it was considered false until further notice. Case closed.

But so far, Joy had had little luck in that department. And proof was overrated anyway, she'd decided. For instance, she could never prove to her parents that Winsome Elementary was an awful place, and as such, the source of her life's misery. Nonsense, they said. They had seen with their own eyes how new and clean the school was, and full of happy children. They'd shaken hands with smiling teachers brimming with enthusiasm, and had read the weekly school newsletters about all of the terrific things going on. All proof that it was a fine school to anyone reasonable.

But as Joy grew older, she often found that what seemed "reasonable" to everyone else seemed completely insane to her. And that's exactly how Darlington seemed—insane. But it just wasn't something she could explain to her parents. It wasn't something that could be measured or captured or documented in any way. There could never be any proof.

And so, no, she couldn't prove there really was a monster in the yard either. And yes, she did admit to herself it did seem a little coincidental that on the very night after staying up late reading about just such a creature that one came snuffling under her window.

But so what? Did the intrepid Dr. Ingram, recurrent hero of *The Compleat and Collected Works of E. A. Peugeot*, need proof before leaping clear of the snapping jaws of some awful monster? Or wait for peer approval before throwing a bundle of dynamite into the portal to some hellish underworld?

"Joy!" repeated Byron. "Are there really such things as bog fiends?"

"I hope so," she muttered.

Joy and Byron walked on, past the spiked walls of the cemetery. Fizz had settled down, busily sniffing the earthy scents of autumn. A raven suddenly called out, and Fizz's head disappeared into the safety of Joy's satchel. At last they arrived at the top of the winding road.

It was difficult to walk at a comfortable pace down such a steep incline, so they found themselves running most of the way, until their feet began stinging on impact. They arrived at the bottom, legs burning and out of breath, and rested by the road for a few minutes before continuing on.

The woods were still and no longer buzzing with insects, thanks to the onset of cooler weather. With the leaves all fallen, Joy and Byron weren't sure where the living trees stopped and the dead ones of the bog began. Which was dangerous, as lakes of foul water hid under layers of peat moss that looked thick enough to stand on, but most certainly were not, as Byron had once proved, sinking with a sploosh up to his armpits.

Joy had been quick to yank him out that day. The water was full of bloodsucking leeches, she knew, having often marveled as their tapered black shapes boiled under the surface like pasta in some dark satanic pot. Byron, drenched and shivering, had whimpered quietly as Joy examined his chunky legs and pale torso, but luckily, not a single leech had managed to latch onto his flesh. They were probably upset about missing an awesome meal like Byron's goose-pimply butt,

Joy had teased as she let go of the elastic on his underwear with a snap.

This time, Byron wasn't taking any chances, prodding ahead of himself with a long stick. Joy kicked herself for forgetting the aquarium net again. A leech would make a pretty cool pet, she thought. But what would she feed it? Would it be happy sucking on something a bit fleshy like a peach? She wasn't sure. Anyway, Fizz would probably just bark at it all day.

Joy let Fizz out, and he hopped happily after them on his leash. Leaves crunched underfoot as they marched into the bog. Moss carpeted the bog in blood red, and an eerie mist swirled in the distance.

Suddenly there came a wailing, high-pitched and blood-curdling. Their two heads spun in opposite directions.

Joy signaled her brother and began scrambling up a mossy hummock, Fizz skidding behind her. Byron crawled quickly after, heart pounding. He caught up with her crouched at the top behind a rotted tree stump.

Peering down, they saw something below, squatting in a clearing. It had wild hair and a black body, wrapped up in what looked like a tarantula's web, and was digging furiously at the base of a tree. Joy turned and held a finger to her lips. She then went to reel in Fizz, finding an empty collar on the end of his leash. The little slimy brat had slipped out again, she realized.

The creature's voice rose steadily, becoming more shrill by the second, like a squawking bird with a serious grudge against a squeaky chew toy. It was the most horrible sound he had ever heard, thought Byron, clamping his hands over his ears.

Joy then spotted Fizz, hopping down toward the clearing. Staying low, she quickly crawled out after him. He stopped, sitting up on his hind legs. Joy reached for him, just as his yellow throat ballooned. It was too late. Fizz began barking. Loudly.

"Who's there?" the creature shrieked in a human voice, whirling around. It was an old woman, they now saw, wearing a black coat wrapped up in a filthy shawl, her long gray hair tangled with bits of leaves and twig, and her blazing eyes darting in their deep sockets as they scoured the foliage for intruders. Clenched in her dirty fingers was a long, gleaming knife.

And she'd spotted them.

CHAPTER 5

Oh, hello, children!" said the old woman. "You scared me half out of my rubber boots!" She had a pleasant lilting voice with a strong accent and wore a friendly if somewhat gnarly-looking smile.

"So sorry," said Joy from a prone position. She clamped a hand on Fizz and reattached his collar, making sure to adjust it one hole tighter. Over her shoulder, Byron peeked out from the safety of the petrified stump as Joy smiled back. "We were just wondering where all the beautiful singing was coming from."

"Oh my! Or what the heck was making such an awful racket, more likely," chuckled the old woman. She folded the knife and dropped it along with some freshly cut herbs into a pocket on the front of her skirt. "How embarrassing! I don't usually have an audience for my little operas, you know." A tufted eyebrow suddenly arched in surprise. "Is that a froggy you've got there on a leash?"

"His name is Fizz," said Joy, brushing dirt from the front of her coat as she stood. "He thinks he's a bulldog," she added, gingerly making her way down the muddy slope to the clearing.

"I see. That explains his curious barking then. And the spikes on his collar."

Joy shrugged. "We've learned it's better just to humor him," she said as Byron arrived, crashing painfully into her back.

"What are your names, bambini?"

"I'm Joy, and this is my brother, Byron."

"Joy, how pretty. And Byron, what a strong name. Do you know what it means?" she asked Byron, who shook his head as he stared back mistrustfully. "*Bear.* Of course, you look more like a chubby teddy at the moment, but in time, I am sure you will be just as noble and powerful. . . . You may call me Madame Portia," she said with a flourishing bow.

"Pleased to meet you," replied Joy with an unintended curtsey. The old woman did look surprisingly regal, despite her considerable filthiness.

Byron, meanwhile, continued to stare at her suspiciously. He'd read the fairy tales, and such chumminess usually meant a kid-size oven was preheating somewhere nearby.

"And what wonders might life have in store for you? Let me see." Madame Portia took one of Joy's hands and turned her palm up. "How unconventional you are, my dear! It says here that you are smart, inquisitive, and romantic," she said, tracing a line with a dirty nail. "And the strong fork here to the Mount of Venus suggests you have a penchant for musical and literary pursuits—that may lead to celebrity. . . . But here it warns not to give into temptation, otherwise everything will be lost."

The old woman released her hand, which now felt unusually hot, Joy noticed.

"And as for you, young man," continued Madame Portia as she unwrapped Byron's tight fist, "it says here you are noble, courageous, and loyal, and will also have a lot of adventures. And look," she added with a giggle, "it says here you are quite the little love bird!"

Byron snatched back his hand, glowering.

"You both have very long life lines. Which means you should live to be a hundred at least."

"Cool," said Joy.

"And so, tell me, you've come today to enjoy one of the most beautiful sphagnum peat moss bogs in the whole world, have you?"

"Yes, we have," answered Joy. "It's nice here."

"Nice?" squawked Madame Portia in horror. "What a pitiful word—'nice.' Natural forces both incredible and mysterious have colluded to create an impossible haven of life within an extraordinary cathedral of death, and you remark, 'It's nice.'" The old woman's face twisted with disgust.

"I am sorry," said Joy carefully.

"Don't worry about it," Madame Portia replied casually. "Now come quick! I want to show you something *too cute!*" The old woman took off at speed, shawl flapping. Joy followed as fast as she could, towing Byron's dead weight behind her. They finally caught up at the edge of a rusty brown pool.

"See him?" whispered Madame Portia, pointing. A few feet away, a large dark shape moved through the water like some armored aquatic monster.

"Yeah!" answered Joy, trying to contain her volume despite her considerable excitement. "What is it?" she asked, adjusting Byron's head slightly so he could see.

"Why, that's Ernesto!"

"Ernesto?" Joy repeated.

"The most spectacular snapping turtle in the bog! Ernesto's very shy, so you are very lucky to see him. But you'd be less lucky to encounter him on land—he is quite a tough customer. He weighs at least seventy-five pounds!"

Joy clamped a hand over Fizz's eyes, just in case he thought of trying his luck.

"This is a very rare and precious ecosystem, you know," Madame Portia said, leaning over. Byron recoiled from her sharp breath, which smelled like a stiff breeze blowing across a field of sodden weeds. "Do you know what other unusual creatures make their homes inside?"

Joy's eyes widened hopefully. "Monsters?"

Madame Portia let out a birdlike shriek. Ernesto vanished with a splash. "You have quite the imagination, young lady," she said laughing. Then her expression turned serious. "To most creatures *we* are the monsters, you know. Monsters who destroy their beautiful homes to make shopping malls and parking lots and golf courses. Monsters who turn a spring rain into toxic acid, and a summer breeze into poisonous smog."

Joy agreed. A hundred years ago, E. A. Peugeot had said the same thing—that the most dangerous monster of all was humankind. But she bit her lip in frustration as Madame Portia changed the subject.

"My husband, Ludwig, rest his soul, was a famous naturalist," said Madame Portia. "He spent his life studying the bog, publishing many articles on its native flora and fauna. That's why we built our home here, to be close to his work."

"You live *here*?" asked Joy in disbelief. "In the bog?"

"You don't believe me? Come and see for yourself. I think I may even have a few gingerbread cookies somewhere for you."

"Sure," said Joy. Byron flashed her a look of alarm.

They followed Madame Portia along an uneven trail. Joy happily imagined Dr. Ingram hobbling across the same scene, his wound black and bubbling as Dickson's awful screams were suddenly silenced by the sound of tearing flesh and snapping bones. She glanced over her shoulder at the dark, tangled woods, shivering deliciously to imagine the possibility that something hellish was stalking them at this very moment.

Meanwhile, Byron was lost in dark thoughts of his own, which he was most certainly not enjoying. Did Hansel feel this way, he wondered, holding Gretel's hand as the witch led them deeper into the forest? He realized that he wasn't sure what he was more afraid of: a hideous death at the hands of some geriatric cannibal, or the embarrassment of suddenly taking off screaming. But if the climactic moment should come anyway, would he finally define himself as the little hero of the story, or just something juicy to be slow-roasted with onions and carrots?

"Here, bambini!" exclaimed Madame Portia, stopping

suddenly. "I want to show you a few meat-eating monsters!" The children skidded to a halt. Byron leaped back into a defensive posture. "No need to be afraid, young man!" said Madame Portia. "That is, unless you are a silly little insect with a sweet tooth."

"What are they called?" asked Joy, crouching beside the ghostly patch of tubular plants. "And why should bugs be afraid of them?"

"They are *Sarracenia illuminus*. The throats of these elegant fellows are coated with nectar, you see. When a little bug climbs inside for a taste, tiny hairs draw it down to be digested." Madame Portia beamed. "A wonderful sugar-coated death."

"Wow," said Joy, looking closer at the mint green veins running up their length. "It's so beautiful—almost electric!"

"You should see *Sarracenia illuminus* at night—how she glows! It's one of the many inhabitants of this bog documented by my late husband, the great and talented Ludwig Zweig. To my great regret, many of his most astounding discoveries were never published before he died! The world is so much the more ignorant as a result!"

"Can't you publish his research yourself?" suggested Joy.

"That's the thing. For all Ludwig was a man of science, he was not only quite disorganized but more than a bit superstitious—both qualities I am sure I only encouraged, I'm afraid. Anyway, he developed this fear of photocopiers, which he believed could somehow 'collate a person's soul' as he put it, so he never made copies of his research," explained Madame Portia. "Now most of his notes are gone and I have no idea where he sent them off to! I can only hope that someone will still come to investigate his latest incredible specimen. What if people think he is just some kook and they toss out his life's work?"

"What kind of incredible specimen?" demanded Joy, unable to check her excitement. "A creature of some sort?"

"Oh, I couldn't say, bambina!" said Madame Portia. "Not before someone comes to verify Ludwig's discovery, that is. Otherwise some charlatan is sure to steal the credit!" Madame Portia grabbed Joy by the shoulders. "I beg you, child, never speak of this to anyone!"

Joy chewed her lips in frustration. Was it the bog fiend Madame Portia was talking about? Here she was, so close to finding out the truth! But the old woman wasn't budging. Joy would have to try a different approach—getting her to give away the location of its den.

"Madame Portia," said Joy lightly, as if changing the subject. "I was wondering if you could tell us how to identify different types of mushrooms."

"Mushrooms? There must be hundreds of species in the bog alone. . . ."

"What about poisonous ones? Where might you find some around here?"

"Oh, I wouldn't go fooling around like that, little miss. Some of them are very dangerous!"

"But—"

"No buts—I won't be party to a death by mushroom. Remember," chided Madame Portia with a wagging finger, "we are in a sphagnum bog, not your corner grocery.

My advice is to pick some up at a supermarket like everybody else. You can find all sorts of fancy ones these days: portobello, oyster, shiitake, you name it." They began walking again, Joy squirming in frustration as Madame Portia marveled aloud at all the amazing varieties of lettuce now available. "Anyway, here were are. Home sweet home."

Joy and Byron both gasped.

Standing on stilts above a black lake was a cigar-shaped structure covered in moss. Brass portholes lined its exterior and a shingled tower rose from the roof. All over, stringy vegetation dangled from what appeared to be rusty scientific instruments. Madame Portia's house looked for all the world like a washed-up submarine from some ancient but technologically underestimated civilization.

"Impressive, si? Ludwig built it. He was good with his hands—and they were oh so strong," said Madame Portia wistfully. "He was once a submariner, you know. That is, until a depth charge sunk his vessel, and his career, when he was just sixteen. Which is also why he was deaf in one ear—he was sleeping with one side of his head pressed up against the hull when the charge went off, the poor darling. Anyway, he could never live in a wooden box after that, not after roaming the great big Atlantic in such a cozy metal tube, he said.

"But it's too much work for me now. I suppose it won't fall down, at least until I am nice and comfortably dead. Now come on, children, come inside. . . ."

Curiosity even got the better of Byron, so he followed Joy and Madame Portia up a swaying gangway leading to the tower. As the old woman swung open the heavy door, there was the sound of scuffling, and the children spotted something scurry out of view as they entered.

"You'll have to excuse the rats—I'm having trouble keeping them out lately," said Madame Portia. "I think they are getting in through Ludwig's old scuba tube," she added, pointing to a shaft located rather precariously in the center of the living room. On one side, Joy saw a ladder descending into the darkness. "Did I mention Ludwig was a keen diver?"

"A scuba diver?" asked Joy, surprised. "In the bog?"

"Oh, yes. Much of his research was performed underwater in fact, so he could observe its inhabitants up close. The pond below us is quite deep in spots, with many remarkable specimens, not to mention old relics."

"Relics?" asked Joy. "What kind of relics?"

"Oh, the bog has swallowed up all manner of things over the centuries, even an entire railway stop that once stood at the foot of Spooking Hill. And many little objects, just like this," said Madame Portia, handing Joy something from an ornately carved desk.

"A pen?"

"An antique stylograph pen, actually," she answered. "Ludwig found it right out there, poking out of the muck on the bottom of the pond."

Joy's eyes lit up. The onyx pen had a gold-plated snake curling around its cap. "Cool!" she exclaimed.

"You like it? You can keep it."

"Really?"

"Of course! Ludwig fished many such things from the black depths of our backyard. I am glad to be rid of the clutter, frankly."

"Thank you so much!" said Joy gratefully. She squeezed it to detect the faint hum of its previous owner. Who could have used such a distinctive thing, and how did it end up in a blood-sucking swamp?

"By the way, Madame Portia, how could your husband go diving down there with all those leeches?"

"My dear, leeches are quite unable to chew their way through a scuba suit, try as they might. Ludwig got the occasional one inside his flipper, but other than that, he was fine. In fact, he said there was nothing more delightful than lying on the bottom, looking up at the blue sky through an angry school of the little devils.

"But I must get some plywood to cover it up now. I don't think I'll be going for a swim myself any time soon. Oh, you wouldn't happen to know any licensed divers interested in purchasing a scuba tank and respirator?"

"I don't think so," said Joy.

"Well, no matter. I can always put it in the classifieds, although it breaks my heart to do it after what happened. Poor Ludwig drowned, you know, just out front there. One wrong step and—splish!—the world lost one of its last true intellects. If only he'd been wearing his scuba gear at the time!"

Madame Portia became wracked with sobs. The children waited awkwardly, with Joy drawing a blank on anything comforting to say.

"Anyway, don't mind the rats," Madame Portia continued finally, wiping her nose with a dingy handkerchief. "They are quite timid, most of the time. They are mainly just interested in getting into the pantry. Speaking of which, I promised you cookies! Excuse me, I'll just be a moment."

Joy and Byron waited, looking nervously for rodents. The sitting room was jammed with cushioned furniture vomiting its stuffing onto the floor. The curved walls were lined with elaborately built bookshelves. They rose over Joy and Byron like cresting waves, crowded with volumes held in place over their heads with leather straps.

"Our library," said Madame Portia fondly as she returned, carrying a tray with two glasses of milk, a plate, and a box that said CHOCOLATE CHUNKS in letters so faded they were barely legible. "Would you believe it, I am completely out of the gingerbread kind!"

Joy scanned the collection of books. *Freaks of Nature: A Study of Botanical Abnormality. The Wild World of Wood Lice. The Idiot's Guide to Being Psychic.*

"Come, come! Here are the cookies you were clamoring for, children," Madame Portia said, putting the tray down and pouring out a heap of shattered pieces. Through the corner of his eye, Byron saw a rat bolt across a section of open floor.

"*The Compleat and Collected Works of E. A. Peugeot!*" cried Joy, pulling the book out. It was a modern edition with its corners chewed off, but it was otherwise the exact same book she owned.

"Oh, I picked that up at a garage sale a long time ago,"

said Madame Portia. "Is it any good? I'd quite forgotten about it, actually."

"Oh yes!" Joy was beaming. "It's my favorite book in the whole world. The author, E. A. Peugeot, was a very famous horror writer who actually lived very near to here, you know." Joy blushed, thinking how her theory had gone down the last time. "At least *I* think so," she added with a shrug. "It hasn't really been proved yet."

Madame Portia laughed. "Well, I wouldn't be surprised. The area has quite a fascinating history, and has been home to more than a few unusual characters, as I know personally. And it's refreshing to see some Darlington children taking an interest in our local heritage."

"We don't live in Darlington," corrected Joy, her eyes flashing angrily at the suggestion. "We're from Spooking."

"Really?" gasped Madame Portia. "Forgive me! It's been a good many years since I was last up the hill to visit my old home, what with no car and this hip, and before that the old town had been long without youngsters. They all grew up and moved on, you see, instead of staying to raise families of their own. Such a pity!" Madame Portia clasped Byron's chin in her filthy hands. "But now there's a new generation of Spooking children, you tell me! How wonderful!"

"*Spooziees*," murmured Byron, his jaw held painfully shut in her grasp.

"Pardon?"

"Spookys," repeated Joy. "It's what they call us down at Winsome Elementary. In Darlington, where we go to school."

"Bah," said Madame Portia. "I wouldn't pay any attention to them," she purred, smoothing Byron's hair. "Spooking will still be standing up on that hill when Darlington is but a melted pool of plastic. Cities like that are obscenities upon nature, and nature won't abide such a thing for long.

"But never mind that. I always look forward to reading a book that comes with such a high recommendation."

Joy handed her back the copy. "I think you will especially like the story 'The Bawl of the Bog Fiend.' And I would actually love to talk to you more about it sometime. But we really should be getting home now."

"What about your milk and cookies?" asked the old woman.

"I'm afraid the rats already helped themselves to them," replied Joy.

Madame Portia turned and saw the now empty plate and two rats cheerfully lapping up the last of the milk. "You dirty, dirty things!" she shrieked. The rats shot under the sofa, knocking over one of the glasses and shattering it.

The children said good-bye. Joy promised to return again soon. Madame Portia said they were welcome any time.

They began making their way home. It was starting to rain and Byron's stomach was growling. He asked Joy if she had brought any food on this expedition.

"Nope, sorry. I forgot."

Byron asked crankily how come Joy always remembered to bring her various weapons, but always forgot to pack some sandwiches.

"Actually, I didn't bother bringing a weapon this time,"

she said. "No point against a bog fiend." They retraced their steps back to the road, passing through a patch of ghostly-looking birch trees. "It's so magical, this place," she sighed. "I can see why someone would want to live here, although I'm not sure I could handle the rats. At least we're lucky to live close enough to visit whenever we want."

"I wonder what it will look like after the bulldozers come."

"Bulldozers?" Joy stopped. It was raining harder now, heavy drops exploding as they stepped out on the paved road. "What do you mean? What bulldozers?" she said over the noise.

"The bulldozers that are coming to clear the bog so they can start major excommunication," answered Byron, thinking that didn't sound exactly right. He shrugged. "And the drainage."

"Byron, what on earth are you talking about?"

"What they were talking about in the boy's washroom after assembly. The man with the loud voice, and the other one."

"The mayor?" asked Joy, alarmed. "You heard him say something about the bog?"

"They came in when I was in the toilet. I heard them talking about how they couldn't start bulldozing until they got something crazy out of the bog." Byron's eyes widened. "Do you think they were talking about your monster maybe?"

Joy's blood went cold. It suddenly all made sense.

"The Misty Mermaid Water Park!" she exclaimed.

"Those Darlington maniacs are going to build it over Spooking Bog! Byron, we've got to stop them!"

Just then a car whizzed passed them, screeching to a halt as the sky opened up completely.

"Joy! Byron!" called Mrs. Wells from the open door. The children ran up. "What on earth are you doing out in the rain without your ponchos?" she asked as they climbed in among the groceries. "Please don't tell me you were in that bog again, Joy Wells. . . ."

"We didn't go in that far," answered Joy, her hair now dark and dripping. Byron didn't comment, having already opened a box of crackers and stuffed his mouth full.

"It's much too dangerous to go in at all," said Mrs. Wells crossly. "I thought we'd talked about this already. If you want to play in the woods, we have a perfectly fine park in town."

"Yes, Mother."

"Now, let's get you both home before you get pneumonia," said Mrs. Wells, stomping the gas. The car shot up the crooked road as streams of rainwater rushed down to meet them. "I still can't believe you forgot your new ponchos on such a day," she said disapprovingly.

CHAPTER 6

It always came in the dead of night. The dreaded visitor. Phipps would wake with a start at its first feathery touch, then feel its crushing weight bearing down on his chest.

It was Death—its relentless approach. At the darkest hour, just when his limbs felt lightest, his eyes would suddenly snap open.

He was going to die.

So what, he scoffed. *Everyone is going to die.* And it did make him smile to think that in a world so unfair, there was one great equalizer—that it would all vanish one day like a puff of smoke for everyone.

But no, he remembered, dying wasn't the issue. The issue was vanishing without a trace, having made no mark on the world. Quickly forgotten even by the few who'd known him. He would toss and turn as the room turned a gloomy blue that recalled the many gray dawns he'd spent in Spooking Cemetery.

At which point, he would throw off the covers and stomp to the shower. Then, rinsing soap and fatigue from his stinging eyes, he would begin plotting again. Plotting against fate.

And so the morning had begun again. It was time to pay another visit to the bog, he decided, as he knotted his tie.

※ ※ ※

Phipps hadn't been back since that terrible afternoon. He had gone to see the old couple to ask them to be reasonable. He'd intended to tell them that the mayor had authorized a nice check to help with moving expenses. He'd meant to point out that there were many other fetid habitats around where a quaint little hermit couple could live.

But somehow it didn't go that way.

He'd approached undetected, finding the old man alone, sketching some sad-looking weed against a backdrop of bog water. The old man had been whistling to himself, a tuneless torrent of notes that refused to conform itself to any sort of musical phrase. He'd seemed completely at ease, without a care in the world.

The cacophony had been enough to ignite a flare of anger in Phipps. Why was he even indulging this lunatic? He had tried diplomacy before and it had failed. It was now time to make the old coot squirm on the point of a hook.

"Gottfried Leibniz!" he had called out cheerfully, emerging from the trees.

The old man jumped with fright. His notebook landed with a splash in front of him.

"Oh dear, I made you drop your drawing," Phipps said, strolling up with a smirk. "I hadn't meant to startle you. I was just remarking what an interesting name you provided me, even if it was false."

The old man's eyes blazed with anger as he retrieved his notebook, which was a complete sodden mess. "What do you want?"

"Oh, I'm just here for a scholarly chat. Did you know who Gottfried Leibniz was? Of course you did, as I can tell you're an educated man. Living like a pig in a swamp, I might add, but I'm sure you worked long and hard for that privilege.

"I, on the other hand, went to music school," he continued, "where I also worked hard but unfortunately didn't learn anything of any use—except how to use a library, that is.

"Which is where I learned that Gottfried Leibniz was a famous German mathematician and philosopher, born in 1646. And of his many observations—most of which I skimmed through yawning—he had one rather interesting belief. Namely that we live in the best of all possible worlds.

"Unfortunately, it didn't fly with his fellow eggheads. This world, they laughed? With all the war and plague and poverty?

"Yes, said Leibniz. Because God is perfect, and perfect beings like Him wouldn't get out of bed to make a world unless it was the best they could do. What do you think? Do you believe we live in the best possible world?"

"I most certainly do not," said the old man. "And I also don't believe you have the right to come on private property asking such flippant questions, Mr.—what was it again?"

"The name is Phipps. You see, I have nothing to hide by claiming to be Albert Einstein. And I must protest—this is not your property. It is public land, administered by the City of Darlington. Of which I am emissary, as I explained."

"That is where you are wrong, Einstein. There are three acres that are private property, and have been so for a hundred years before it was inherited by me. It is upon those three acres that my home now stands, as I keep explaining."

"But since there is no such deed on record at City Hall under the name of Leibniz, which was nothing more than a childish prank on your part, I'm afraid I can't just take your word for it. Either show me a deed or vacate. This land has been rezoned for development."

"Development," the old man had spat. "This bog has developed for a hundred thousand years without your help. Bah, you know nothing. Do you have any idea what kind of ancient specimen dwells here? Living in shadow, untouched by human meddling for untold millennia?"

"Don't tell me. A rat as big as a dachshund? Or a frog the size of a poodle?"

The old man had laughed. "No, but by coincidence, you just named two mainstays of its diet." The old man had gazed toward the dark interior of the bog. "No, what lurks within that tangle of fossilized forest there is much more amazing. And once the scientific community learns of it, this bog will take its place among the ecological treasures of this planet. So you can rezone your development right up—"

"Well, I hope you've managed to save a couple of those nice little drawings then, because in a matter of a month, we're flattening everything around here."

The old man's eyes had flashed. "You wouldn't dare. . . ."

"Watch me."

It had been Phipps's plan to then turn on his heel and leave the old fool to chew over the apocalypse coming soon to his pathetic mud-hole. Instead he'd found himself going purple as a pair of powerful old hands crushed his windpipe.

But surprised though Phipps had been, he was no stranger to violence. It was an old occupational hazard from the days when making music was a dangerous business, when he'd been kicked, punched, and pelted with bottles more times than he remembered. So despite his shock and dwindling supply of oxygen, he was taking none of it from some liver-spotted little skinhead. He'd punched the old man hard in the stomach, then unleashed a flurry of strikes at the old man's head.

But there'd been no effect—the old man had held tight. Phipps's windpipe had by then felt like a toilet paper tube under a truck tire. Then his vision had darkened and his knees had begun buckling.

Suddenly the old man had let go, letting out a horrible rattling gasp. Clutching his chest, he'd stumbled backward, before crashing through the peat moss into the black bog water below.

Phipps had fallen to his knees. He'd struggled to inhale, his throat aflame as if phantom hands were still crushing it. Through the optical fireworks celebrating his near-fatal asphyxiation, Phipps had glimpsed a horrifying sight: a hand, encrusted with leeches, clawing desperately at the sphagnum. Then he'd blacked out, falling face-first into the mud.

By the time he'd regained consciousness, it had been too late. The hand had gone completely still.

Phipps had stood up unsteadily before staggering out of the bog.

Now he returned to the horrible spot. The sphagnum showed no sign of having been disturbed in the slightest, much less swallowing a man alive kicking and screaming. At the end of the path, the old man's bizarre house sat silently on its stilts.

Phipps approached quietly. As usual, the overgrown house was in total gloom. A single light burned inside, he noticed, tiptoeing up the slippery gangway.

There she was, just a few feet away from where he hung over the rail peeking through the porthole.

She was sitting under a standing lamp. Beyond, shadows scuttled across the carpet. She was reading a book.

Phipps imagined the old woman returning home on that fateful day, with her husband's heart pills or a few groceries perhaps. Crying out as she spotted the glint of a wedding ring in the sphagnum.

Poor old Portia—the Mysterious and Amazing Madame Portia, as the painted sign over her shop once read. Now just another little old widow filling up her days before oblivion.

She hadn't even recognized him, or so it had seemed when he came to give her and her new toadlike husband notice to clear off. But then again, it had been twenty-five years since he'd last spoken to her. He had been only sixteen back then. A shy boy, he had been, busy fixing instruments and digging graves.

How exotic she'd seemed to him, he remembered, and beautiful. All the women of Spooking flocked to her candlelit shop for furtive glimpses into their uncertain futures. Even today, he could still remember the cracked tailpiece of the violin he fixed for her. The very one she played not long after while he swung the heavy shovel, installing her first husband—the crazy clock maker—into the cold Spooking earth to tick away the seconds as he turned into dust.

Now here was the Mysterious and Amazing Madame Portia: gray, dirty, and living in a bog. *What a pity*, he thought. Wouldn't she be so much happier in a nice rest home, reading tea leaves and casting spells over the other wrinkled residents, maybe going for husband number three? How could she go on living alone in this awful place? He sighed, feeling himself fill with uncommon sympathy.

But then Phipps saw what the old woman was reading, and the tiny light of fondness winked out.

It was the infernal work of the accursed Peugeot himself. The famous son, the beloved one, whose vile deed was still being punished a century later. He squinted, making out the familiar title at the top of the bookmarked page: "The Bawl of the Bog Fiend."

Ah, yes. Wherein a slumbering swamp monster is disturbed by Dr. Ingram and his pathological inability to leave well enough alone; unleashing horror, suffering, and death on the procession of fools who never fail to follow him like a litter of trusting puppies. Nice work, Doctor! The scientific community would owe you a debt of gratitude, were your findings not always disregarded as the hysterical ramblings of someone gone completely insane.

How unbelievable, Phipps thought, that not a single tale ever reached its logical conclusion, with the good doctor having his fat meddling face ripped off. But then what bumbling idiot would take up the cause of luring hapless assistants and innocent townsfolk into yet another snarling maw in the next installment?

Behind him there was a crack, then a crash. Phipps jumped. Just a rotten branch, he told himself. The bog went deathly still again. How could she stay here, he wondered? Reading that creepy schlock?

He knocked on the door.

From inside came the sound of mad scuttling. After a pause, a voice demanded: "Who's there?"

"The City of Darlington, Madame. No need for alarm."

The door opened. "You again," said Madame Portia testily. "And since you are not here to sell me a violin, you must be here to bury me," she said, folding her arms. "Well, I am not dead yet, as you can see."

Phipps cocked an eyebrow in surprise. "You remembered me all along?" He smiled. "So my hurt feelings were quite unnecessary."

"I am not completely away with the fairies, you know," she replied defensively. "I just didn't want to bring it up in front of Ludwig. I tried not to reminisce too much about Spooking in his presence, you see, as imagining my previous life with my first husband always put him in a black mood. For all his wonderful qualities, dear Ludwig was quite jealous."

"I see."

"But I should say that even in your fancy suit and tie, you still look like the same little boy to me," she added, sneakily taking a hold of his hand and glancing at his palm.

"I'm flattered, Madame," said Phipps warmly, despite his secret irritation. "The truth is that the little boy you remember has been around the block a few too many times now." She suddenly dropped his hand like it was on fire.

"Oh yes, so much experience out there in the great big world, hmm?" she asked, her eyes flashing with pity before turning back to polished stone. "It was just a shame you broke your poor mother's heart, leaving home like that. For what, awful ear-splitting rock music? Well, that's the curse of your generation—it's not what you do with your life, but whether you'll become famous doing it."

Phipps chuckled. "What perceptive commentary! Really, you should have a column in the newspaper or something. But that is the least of my curses, as I'm sure you're aware. Or was it not obvious on my palm?"

"Sadly, yes."

"But you can be of no help, of course."

Madame Portia sighed. "The truth is, I'm not that sort of gypsy. Their kind passed on in your great-great-grandfather's time, taking the secrets of their evil eyes and hexes with them. I can only glimpse the future—I have no power over the past."

"Is that so?"

"Yes, it is. If I did, I would have helped your father, believe me. Your mother was one of my best customers! What a lovely woman, she was. She asked for my help too, but it was no use."

"Perhaps you can try again," suggested Phipps. "Have a look at a few old books, cards, scrolls—whatever you can find. Then maybe we can come to a happier arrangement about all this," he said, motioning around him at the bog.

Madame Portia breathed out heavily. "My dear, I am a soothsayer. The burden I carry is telling others what is revealed to me. To forewarn of what is to come. Not to bring comfort or give false hope. I cannot alter fate. I can only counsel others to make peace with fate. This is what I did for your mother and father. And they were at peace."

"Being in denial is not peace!" replied Phipps angrily. "Is this what years of staring into a crystal ball teaches you? That life is a spectator sport? Well you're wrong! Fate is not something to let run over you—it is something to rage against! To bend to your will, to do your bidding!"

"There you are wrong," said Madame Portia. "The more you run from destiny, the quicker its pursuit. Look at your father, how his faithfulness and cheer delayed his vanishing. The deeds of which you speak only accelerate the end, my dear."

"I beg to differ," he said, his voice quavering. "But I see you won't help."

"I'm afraid I can't."

"Then I will continue to pursue whatever courses are available to me," he said viciously. "Some of which you won't much like, I might add."

"I don't need a crystal ball to say it comes as little surprise," replied Madame Portia coldly. "Especially not after how you left your mother all alone like that. Did you know I arranged her burial all by myself? Which isn't very easy to do up in Spooking these days."

"What did you expect, for me to dig the hole myself?" Phipps spat.

"Maybe. Or perhaps just to attend her burial like a good son."

"Enough," he interrupted. "I didn't trudge all this way to get guilt trips from an old gypsy. I have come on city business, to let you know that we've looked through all the records and there is no deed for any property in the name of Ludwig Zweig. That being the case, I no longer have any need to seek your cooperation, since you are trespassing. The bog will be destroyed and this illegal structure along with it. So I suggest you gather your effects."

"Do you see that thing on top of my house?" asked Madame Portia defiantly.

Phipps glanced up suspiciously at the device she was pointing at, which was covered in a thick layer of moss. "Yes. What is it?" he asked wearily.

"It's a satellite dish that Ludwig set up. Beaming one hundred and fifty channels into my home with digital clarity and CD-quality sound!"

"And?"

"And my favorite channel is something called the Justice Network. Do you watch it? All police shows and legal dramas, twenty-four hours a day. All very realistic and very well researched.

"Anyway, I recently learned—in that show with the pretty blond lawyer raising a child genius on her own—that people in my predicament can assert something called *adverse possession* on a property."

"Adverse *what?*"

"Wait, there was another name . . . Oh yes, I remember now: *squatters' rights*. It turns out that since we have occupied the land for years without challenge, I can make a *hostile claim* on the property. I do love all the legal lingo! You can argue otherwise, which is your *prerogative*, and then the courts will decide. But it will most certainly take some time to present all the evidence, especially since I plan on representing myself, just like that crazy old lady did on that show with the handsome young lawyer who is raising his sister's child—the naughty one—all on his own. Anyway, I can see you are not up on your common law, or don't get cable. . . ."

Phipps had stopped listening to her words, but instead watched her gold tooth flash in the meager light. Oh, he'd heard of squatters' rights all right—he and his band had once lived in an abandoned building for an entire year until they'd accidentally burned the place down. And there had been nothing anyone could do about it.

How easy it would be, he started thinking blackly, to just simply strangle the old woman and toss her body into the black drink below. But that would make him a murderer—

and murderers didn't usually strike while their car was parked out on the shoulder in plain view to anyone passing.

"Madame," he said finally, interrupting her. "You should know you are making a terrible mistake. Squatters' rights or not, you can't stay here any longer."

"Oh, really? And why is that, dear boy?"

"Because it's simply not safe here—not after nightfall," answered Phipps. He walked slowly down the metal gangway, turning at the bottom. "Or didn't your husband tell you? Think—why would he build a home like this, out of rivets and iron?" he called up to her. "It's not safe here. Not at all."

CHAPTER 7

Why me???"

It was a question Joy had asked often, usually shrieked at the sky with mossy gravestones as audience. This time, however, she expected an answer.

"No one else can take your brother to the party," replied Mrs. Wells, pouring out cereal. "I have a staff meeting and your father is with clients all day."

Mr. Wells had left in a state of panic only minutes earlier, his untucked shirt fluttering behind him.

"But it's Sunday—who works on a Sunday?"

"Neither of us are happy about it, believe me, but that's life. What would you have me do, make Byron stay home bored, while you sit with your nose in a book? Just look at his poor little face."

Byron sat with his hands in his lap, devoid of any expression.

"But why do I have to go? Can't you just drop him off and pick him up later?"

"I won't be back in time."

"Then how will we get home?"

"You can get the bus back."

"By ourselves?" Joy gasped in horror.

"Joy, if you're old enough to sneak out in the middle of the night to go wandering around a graveyard, I think you're old enough to take a bus on your own. You are certainly brave enough."

It was the first time Mrs. Wells had mentioned the incident since Joy had been grounded over it earlier in the summer. It had been a clear night under a full moon—a perfect night according to Peugeot to glimpse a shape-shifting werewolf loping through the tall grass, inhaling field mice like popcorn.

As always on such supernatural expeditions, Joy had waited for everyone to be asleep before sneaking out. This occasion, however, she must have unsettled her bedside table lamp making her preparations, as it fell over with a crash sometime after her departure. Discovering Joy's bed empty, her startled parents had bundled the still unconscious Byron into the car and set off in a panicked search of the neighborhood. They'd spotted her flashlight in the cemetery just as she was returning home disappointed.

Joy's parents had not been amused, but it could have been worse. What they didn't know was that Joy had originally planned on taking Byron with her, but couldn't wake him up. Nor did they discover the heavy silver candlestick from the dining room—a precious heirloom, as it was often referred to—stuffed under her sweater as a little werewolf insurance. Werewolves aren't partial to silver, according to Peugeot, nor being conked on the head with it.

"But Byron doesn't even have any friends from Darlington,"

said Joy, changing the subject. "Whose party is it anyway?"

"Lucy Primrose," answered Byron nonchalantly. Joy stared suspiciously at his oddly cocked eyebrow, which he lowered immediately.

"Never heard of her," said Joy, although the name Primrose did sound vaguely familiar. "How do you know she isn't from some family of freaks? A lot of very weird people live down in Darlington, Mum. Doesn't it sound a little suspicious that *Byron* was invited to some prissy little girl's birthday?"

"Joy Wells!" said Mrs. Wells sternly. "There's nothing suspicious about it! Really, you have to stop reading those creepy stories if that's how you're starting to see the world. Everything is not some dark conspiracy. A little girl is having a perfectly ordinary birthday party, and I think it's terrific that Byron's made enough of an impression to be invited."

"The whole class was invited, actually," said Byron.

"But—"

"It doesn't matter, Byron, the point is you were invited."

"But—"

"And if you're any kind of sister at all, you'll take him without another word. You should be thankful to have such a wonderful brother."

"All right!"

Joy looked down at her bowl of cereal, which was now full of soggy, swollen checks of wheat. *Blech.* She did feel guilty. Byron didn't get invited to much after all. He didn't really have friends, even in Spooking. He was too quiet and shy. He just followed Joy wherever she went, playing her games, going on her adventures, and doing pretty much whatever she asked without the slightest complaint. She was lucky to have him. The least she could do was take him to a birthday party.

But a *perfectly ordinary* birthday party, as her mother so precisely put it? It made her shudder.

"Could you also put on a nice dress so you look presentable?" added Mrs. Wells.

❦ ❦ ❦

An hour later they were roaring down the winding road through the woods, and onto the main road through Darlington. Byron stared out the window. Billboards and bus shelters whipped by, glowing with advertisements of pretty people enjoying delicious snacks and refreshing beverages as pouting models wore jeans hanging well below their underwear. Byron's stomach churned. He ran his hand over his hair, checking the side parting held in place with sweet-smelling gel.

The car stopped at a light.

"You look nice in that dress, Joy, but why did you have to ruin it with those hideous boots?" asked Mrs. Wells.

"What's wrong with them?"

"Oh please, Joy. They're motorcycle boots, with steel plates on the front. Not something one would normally pair with a pretty dress. Unless one is trying to punish their mother, that is."

"My little pink ballet slippers are in the wash," protested Joy with a smirk.

Mrs. Wells sighed noisily as she stomped the gas of the

Wells's ancient station wagon, its fake wood paneling a brown streak to onlookers. The rest of the family were convinced that in a former life Mrs. Wells had been either a highway patrolman or a getaway driver—a life that most likely terminated in a fiery crash, they thought uncomfortably.

Its wheels now smoking visibly, the station wagon turned into a large parking lot. They hurtled across the vast grid of empty spaces until they reached a cluster of parked cars in front of a large blue building resembling some sort of castle.

They skidded to a halt.

"Here it is: Kiddy Kingdom. Joy, did I give you the bus money?"

Joy stared in horror at the plywood portcullis that was the front door. Through the glass front doors beyond, she could see someone in a pink helmet waving a pink sword.

Someone please kill me.

"Joy."

"Huh?"

"Do you have the bus money?"

"Yes!"

"Then you can get out of the car."

Byron was waiting outside already, clutching a gift bag stuffed with mint-green tissue paper in one hand while hiking down the waistband of his corduroys with the other. Joy got out and slammed the door.

The passenger window rolled down with a screeching sound. "Have fun!" shouted Mrs. Wells, craning over. "See you at home!" The window whirred up again. Mrs. Wells fast-reversed and executed a squealing spin that turned the car immediately in the opposite direction.

"Let's get this over with," Joy said to Byron. "And pull up your pants, you look ridiculous! What's with that?"

As they headed in, Joy noticed a man in a parked car—a black shiny monster—staring grimly at the entrance, his knuckles white from gripping the steering wheel. He turned, his eyes meeting Joy's. She felt a jolt—she was sure she knew him from somewhere.

They walked on, under the portcullis. Automatic doors opened with a *whoosh*.

"None shall pass!" shouted the pink knight, leaping out. "Unless, that is, ye either best me in a duel or proclaim the name of your king or queen!" The knight then began menacing them with his foam sword.

"Excuse me?" demanded Joy.

Byron slipped in front of her. "Lucy Primrose," he said.

"Ah! Welcome, subjects of Her Royal Highness Princess Primrose," said the pink knight, lowering his sword. "Third door on the left," he added flatly.

Joy led Byron down a long hallway, carefully painted to look like stone. Joy noticed the effect became less and less convincing the farther they walked, until finally it became a simple solid gray. They were greeted by a teenage girl in a medieval dress.

"Court of Primrose?" she asked through clicking bubble gum. "Yes? This way to the Great Hall. Lady Lucy awaits you . . . ," she droned.

The door opened. An awesome sound was unleashed—wild, shrill, and terrible, like an aviary with an unwelcome weasel in its midst. Inside, children ran screaming in every direction. On one side, the boys, having helped themselves to a cache of foam weapons and armor, fought a pitched battle on a medieval-themed plastic jungle gym, with several already injured and writhing on the rubberized mat below. On the other side, the girls, wearing shiny smocks and pointed princess hats, bickered viciously over turns on a mechanical unicorn.

Above it all rose a little girl with fine long hair blazing like an autumn sunset, perched upon a golden throne, tiara shimmering and scepter gleaming as she posed for a crush of adults with miniature video cameras.

Byron was frozen in the doorway, staring at Lucy as she smiled at her assembled subjects. Joy pointed him toward the table buckling under an enormous pile of presents. Byron wound his way through the chaos, looking for a surface on which to set his gift bag. Wedging it in roughly, he joined the party with an awkward smile.

Joy spotted a chair, blissfully away from the action along the wall near the door. With a crumpled tissue from her pocket, she made herself some earplugs. *Much better,* she thought, sitting down. She watched as a costumed employee provided Byron with an orange sword and shield before pushing him headlong into the melee. He got no farther than the little drawbridge. Overwhelmed by green defenders, he vanished from view under raining blows.

Joy had a funny feeling, like she was being watched. She

scanned the crowd, but happily, no one seemed to be paying the slightest attention to her. Then she saw him. His name was Louden Primrose. That's where she had heard the name Primrose before—from her class! Louden sat in a chair against the opposite wall, teetering backward with his arms folded across his chest.

Staring at her with a little smile.

Joy looked away without acknowledging him. In her experience, Darlington boys were all the same: a bunch of brainless obnoxious jerk-faces. Louden, she remembered, could stretch that smile frighteningly ear to ear, which sure made the little Darlington bubbleheads giggle.

She looked back again. He was definitely staring at her. He wasn't smiling now, she noticed, but was busy stifling a yawn. Perhaps like her more regular school tormentors, he was only wishing he could alleviate his boredom by nailing her with an elastic band or hissing "spooky-spooky-spooky" in her face. She began flipping through her mental scrapbook of humiliations for something she could pin on Louden, but drew a blank. Come to think of it, he'd hardly ever even spoken to her.

Louden gave her a little wave. Joy's heart leaped with shock.

Just then a short figure appeared in front of her—a younger boy with a dark bowl cut parted in the center, wearing a little suit and tie. His lips were moving, but he wasn't making a sound, strangely.

There was a swell of noise as Joy suddenly remembered to remove an ear plug. "Can I help you?" she asked.

"I was just saying that you seem a little bit old to be invited to this party."

Joy looked back at the odd boy, dumbfounded. He couldn't have been any older than Byron, but his speaking manner was completely unlike any eight-year-old that Joy had ever met. He spoke more like a grown-up. In fact, she realized, he actually looked a lot like a grown man who had somehow been shrunk in the wash.

"I wasn't invited," she replied. "I'm waiting for it to finish so I can bring my little brother home."

"And who might your brother be?"

"Byron," said Joy. "Byron Wells."

"Ah yes," said the boy. "He's in my class. Good kid." There was a long pause. "By the way, you're right—I'm the guy."

"Pardon?"

"The guy. The winner." He leaned forward. "The one who came up with the idea of the Misty Mermaid Water Park!" His eyebrows flitted up and down. "Except they changed the name on me. I wanted to call it Aqua! Aqua! Aqua! I like things in threes, you see."

Joy then recognized him: He was the boy onstage at the assembly, with Principal Crawley and the Mayor. The City of the Future contest.

"The name's Morris M. Mealey. Again, three M's. Three is a very powerful number, you know. POW. ER. FUL. Three syllables."

"Ah."

"That water park is going to make Darlington the most exciting vacation spot on the seaboard. Did you know that?

We are going to be up to here in tourists," said Morris, karate-chopping himself in the forehead.

"I can't wait," said Joy flatly.

"Look, it's Mr. Phipps!" said Morris, tripping over Joy's boots. "So nice to see you here, sir! To what do we owe the pleasure?"

Joy looked down with annoyance at the scuff Morris had left on the metal plate of one of her boots. Turning angrily, she saw that standing in the doorway was a man, his piercing eyes flashing with disgust at the boy leaping up at him.

It was the man from the car outside—the same man onstage at assembly with Principal Crawley and the Mayor, she suddenly realized.

Except he was now dressed like a complete fool.

CHAPTER 8

A jester! The agency had told him he was to be a wandering minstrel, not some capering fool! The outrage! And who was this little creep? He shot the boy an awful glare that caused the bells on his pointy hat to ring out merrily.

"Mr. Phipps, it's me! Morris M. Mealey, conceiver of the Misty Mermaid Water Park!"

It was all coming back to Phipps now. The contest at the elementary school. Darlington, City of the Future. The self-important little bootlicker with the bowl cut.

Actually, it had been a no-brainer. The Mealey kid had had the only idea they could use, although Phipps had to admit to being partial to the young wit who depicted UFOs laying waste to the area.

He considered for a moment pretending to be someone else, but doubted it would discourage the boy.

"Morris," he finally acknowledged with a stiff smile.

"I didn't realize you were a performer, Mr. Phipps!"

"Only on special occasions."

The special occasion in question was last week's blowing a month's salary on a horse named Cindy's Pride. And how proud Cindy must have felt, as her mighty stallion thundered over the finish line, his jockey left facedown on the far side of the track!

Gambling—or speculating, as Phipps liked to think of it—was an ugly addiction that he just couldn't shake. Which was unfortunate since he considered gamblers a despicable bunch. *Can't you bet on your own talents, you pathetic cowards?* he had wondered, sneering at the screaming spectators before finally tearing his own worthless bet into tiny pieces.

Now he was about to be thrown out of his apartment unless he came up with the rent within a week. It was ridiculous! He was only a couple months late, three at the most. Didn't the landlord realize who he was, and the number of crooked city inspectors and rabid fire marshals he had on speed-dial?

Apparently not. So he needed a gig. Unfortunately, there wasn't a lot of call for avant-garde multi-instrumentalists these days, nor aging punk rockers.

"We do need a wandering minstrel to sing 'Happy Birthday' at Kiddy Kingdom," the agency said over the phone. "The usual guy is getting laser eye surgery tomorrow. It's ten performances total, standard day rate. Interested? Oh, it says here you must be able to provide your medieval-style instrument, like a lute, whatever that is. Got anything that passes for one?"

Passes for one? How insulting! He now opened the case, revealing a beautiful instrument handmade by his own father, a perfect replica of a lute from 1675. No one in this vomit-inducing building was fit to glance at its lustrous finish, he felt, much less be within earshot of its dulcet tones. He'd been forced to make another agonizing trip up the hill for it, finding it among the many other instruments in their dust-caked cases at the back of the derelict shop. As he left, he had pulled the fading FOR SALE sign from the window and tossed it on the floor.

"Whoa, nice guitar, Mr. Phipps," said Morris. "I play a bit of saxophone, actually—"

"It is not a *guitar*," snapped Phipps as he lay its case against the wall beside Joy's chair. "It is a lute. Now would you please excuse me?"

Joy and Morris watched as Phipps waded through the sea of children wearing the grim expression of a sewer worker up to his belt buckle in human waste. He approached one of the teenage employees, who pointed him toward Lucy.

"What a guy, that Mr. Phipps," Morris said to Joy. "He's Mayor MacBrayne's right-hand man, you know. I spoke to him backstage a bit after assembly. He even said I was a natural politician, the way I *fill the air with words*." Morris grinned. "I just love the vision this administration has for Darlington. I was even thinking of maybe heading up the mayor's youth wing to help him campaign for re-election, whenever that is. Are you interested?"

"Interested? In what?"

Morris laughed. "Duh—in becoming a member of Minors for Mayor MacBrayne, of course! I know it's a mouthful, so I was thinking of shortening it to the Triple M's."

Joy shot him the most withering look she could muster from her vast collection of expressions conveying repulsion.

"I'm not joining your stupid club, kid, or anything like it," she said incredulously. "In fact, I happen to think Mayor MacBrayne is a big fat jerk!"

Morris staggered backward as if he'd been slapped. "Wait a second, missy—this big fat jerk, as you call him, is only building a fantastic attraction right on your doorstep!"

"I don't care!" shouted Joy. "The stupid water park—*your water park*—is going to destroy Spooking Bog!"

"Spooking Bog?" Morris looked confused. "Wait, is that where they're going to be building it?"

"Yes!"

"Classic!" Morris laughed. "That's the perfect spot! What geniuses! Hey, c'mon, it's time for the cake."

Morris trotted off toward the crowd forming around Lucy as Joy trembled with frustration at missing the opportunity to choke him by his tie. Phipps stood plucking his lute beside Lucy as a huge, frighteningly aflame birthday cake approached.

"*Happy birthday to you*," Phipps began singing with a melodious voice. Everyone joined in—a hesitant off-key murmur that grew louder and louder with each passing second until it became so painfully noisy and tuneless it sounded like Lucy was being serenaded by a choir of zombies clambering to eat her.

"*Happy birthday, dear Lucy, happy birthday to you . . .*"

Joy sat fuming. She had to get out of there. Where was Byron? She spotted him, hopping up and down, trying to get a view of Lucy blowing out the gathering fireball that was reducing her cake to a pool of bubbling icing. A cheer erupted as a sudden puff of acrid black smoke rose above the line of heads.

Cake, then presents—this was going to take forever! Joy growled to herself, thinking of the boy's smug little face again. *"Classic!"* He didn't care about destroying Spooking Bog, not one bit. And neither would anyone. It was just a bunch of dead trees they drove by.

Joy stared into space, imagining bulldozers tearing through the bog, wrenching up ancient trees and crushing poor Ernesto under their steely tracks. Then she pictured cement trucks barfing load after load over the gaping hole, and towering cranes, an obscene forest of them, hoisting plastic tubes into place for the sunscreen-stinking masses to slide on.

It made her want to scream.

"Did you get a piece?"

It was Louden Primrose.

"Huh?" asked Joy, recoiling. He held out a Styrofoam plate with a thick wedge of cake slathered in pink icing. "Um, no." She felt her neck burning from embarrassment.

"Well, then take this one before the little brats eat it all." He handed her the plate and a plastic fork. "It's not bad actually, compared to last year's at least."

"Thanks," said Joy. Louden shuffled awkwardly, waiting for her to take a bite. Joy sliced through the gooey icing and scooped up a spongy forkful. The sickly sweetness made her face clench as she took a bite, sending electric jolts across her tooth enamel. She was then overcome with the sensation that all the moisture was being sucked from her brain.

"Mmm, good," she managed.

Louden smiled and shrugged, heading off to hand out more. Joy sat stunned, polishing off the rest of the disgusting cake just in case he came back. With a groan, she put the empty plate under her chair. She needed milk or water. She would have drunk any liquid, even gasoline at that point, but there was no way she was going over to the frenzy at the refreshment table.

"Byron!" she barked as he wandered aimlessly within range. He had given up trying to squeeze through a wall of elbows to watch Lucy open her gifts—it was simply impenetrable. "Byron!"

"What?" he asked dejectedly.

"Get me a drink. Anything, so long as it is wet."

Hands in his cords, Byron slunk off toward the refreshments. He was acting weird lately, Joy thought. And not his normal weird—there was something deeply odd about his behavior.

"Excuse me," said a voice. "I need to get my case." Joy looked up. It was the fool—Mr. Phipps, the mayor's right-hand man, as that obnoxious Morris kid had called him. She shuddered.

It wasn't that he was ugly, although he certainly wasn't handsome with his bony face and bulging Adam's apple, blue-black hair, and almost colorless eyes. Up close, she noticed his ears were rimmed with holes—empty piercings—looking like two rounds of cheese nibbled by mice.

But what struck her most was how different he looked,

completely unlike the other grown-ups she came across in Darlington. Like he came from another place—another time—entirely.

Joy found herself suddenly addressing him.

"Did you know," said Joy, clearing her throat, "that Spooking Bog is a very rare and precious ecosystem?"

Phipps crouched by the case, which he had opened, revealing a blue plush velvet interior. He glanced at Joy with disinterest. "Is it?"

"Yes. It's also the home to many unusual species, including snapping turtles that weigh up to seventy-five pounds."

"Fascinating," Phipps answered as he gently laid the lute inside and began cleaning the strings and body with a soft-looking cloth. He then suddenly stopped and turned toward her. "You're not one of those tree-hugging types, are you?"

"No," said Joy unsurely.

"That's good, because once they're on your case, all your hate mail starts reeking of patchouli, which is something I just couldn't handle at the moment."

Joy stared back in bewilderment.

"Sorry. What I meant to say is that I don't quite follow your interest in Spooking Bog," he said with a wide smile. "It is really just a muddy hole, nothing more. And there are plenty of other muddy holes like it where the big turtles can live."

"So it's true you're going to build some mermaid park there."

Phipps raised his eyebrows. "Now, that's something I can't

comment on at this stage, um—what is your name, young lady?"

"Joy."

"Joy," he repeated with amusement, looking at her darkly serious face. "Well, Joy, I will say this: There are a lot of wonderful things coming soon to Darlington, all of which are much more fun than an icky old bog. Did you know you have the privilege of living in one of the best-kept secrets in the country? Sure, Darlington's a bit small now, but it's only getting bigger and better! By the time you are all grown up, it will be an amazing place!"

"I don't live in Darlington. I live in Spooking," replied Joy proudly.

Hearing this, Phipps laughed. It suddenly reminded Joy of a giggling boy she'd once caught pulling the wings off a butterfly.

"Spooking, eh?" said Phipps, closing the spring locks of the case with a snap. He turned, still crouching, and looked at her with his icy blue eyes, studying her face, her hair, and her clothes, it seemed. A shiver tore down Joy's spine. "Okay then, young friend, perhaps you do deserve another explanation. Do you know what a legacy is?"

"Yes."

"Really?"

"It's something left behind by dead people."

"Impressive," he said smiling. "Spooking girls are certainly clever these days."

Joy shrugged. "I learned it from my father—he's a lawyer."

"I see! Well, yes, that's the best kind of legacy, young

lady, made up of valuable things like money and property and titles and so forth. And sometimes there's another kind of legacy, an unwelcome sort handed down to unfortunate future generations who don't want or deserve any part of it. But let's talk about happy legacies, the kind your father handles. Do you have any siblings, may I ask?"

"A brother," Joy answered automatically.

"And what street do you live on, up there in Spooking?"

"Bellevue," she answered, this time lying.

"A fine street! And I imagine you must live in a big old house then."

"I guess."

"Well, did you ever think how one day that house will be yours? It will—it's the legacy your parents will leave to you. Isn't that amazing?"

Joy imagined having the house all to herself. She'd be just like Melody Huxley! With a stab of guilt she then remembered Byron and how her parents would be dead.

"But if things stay as they are, that will never happen," Phipps added darkly. "Your house will crumble into dust long before, along with all the other houses in the neighborhood. And you'll have to move then, except no one will give you even a penny for such a terrible mess. In the end, you and your brother will be left with nothing. Your parents' precious legacy will become completely worthless.

"But what if in the meantime, some wonderful new attraction gets built there?" Phipps continued brightly. "Some sort of big exciting project that brings thousands and thousands of visitors to the area? Like a water park, for instance! Then people will pay a lot of money for a property like yours, no matter what condition it is in. Because the land itself will become valuable! More valuable than your house even, which they could always knock down to build something new. And what happens then? Well, you and your brother will be rich, of course! And then you can move anywhere in the whole world and do anything you please!"

Joy looked back at him without expression.

"Well, what do you think?" asked Phipps. "Doesn't that sound a lot better than spending your whole life stuck in a sad old town that's dying a slow death?"

"Spooking *isn't* dying," hissed Joy through her teeth.

"Oh no? Have you ever seen anyone moving in up there, for example?"

The question took Joy off guard. She'd seen a few moving vans up in Spooking; however, they were always carting stuff away, come to think of it, leaving FOR SALE signs permanently in their wake.

"How about whenever some old resident croaks, passes away, kicks the bucket—does a light ever go on in their house again? Or does it just stay black forevermore?"

Joy stared back silently.

"Precisely," said Phipps, smiling. "To stay healthy, a town needs living, breathing people, not a bunch of rattling ghosts. Spooking is dying. We must get ready to bury it before its foul smell gets on the wind."

Joy ground her teeth together, furious.

"Every child loves their hometown, of course. But the

place you love doesn't really exist anymore," said Phipps. "I'm only trying to make things better. For you, your brother, and any other poor children still up there on that hideous hill. There's no future in Spooking. One day, you won't see the place the way you do now, as it once was. One day, you will see it for what it is.

"And unless someone does something about it now, when that day comes, you will be very, very unhappy."

He grabbed his case and stood up, looking into the girl's eyes, like two burning coals under her furrowed brow. He smiled, knowing exactly what she saw up on that hill.

After all, he'd once seen it too.

He turned with his case and left, bells tinkling.

CHAPTER 9

The bus stop wasn't supposed to be far, according to the directions Mrs. Wells had given them. Joy and Byron first crossed the endless plain of parking lot, dodging the convoys of harried parents bearing away their shrieking, sugar-fueled children. Then the simple instruction to "head over a block" turned out to mean trudging the length of an eighteen-hole golf course.

So it wasn't like Joy's patience was being tested—it was like she had already failed the exam and was rewriting it with a defective ballpoint pen that had to be shaken two hundred times before scratching out a single answer. And Byron's trailing behind with his nose in his loot bag wasn't helping.

"Come on, I don't want to miss the next one!" she shouted back. But it was too late. They arrived just as the Number 6 pulled away, leaving them in a cloud of diesel fumes.

"Great!" declared Joy, not knowing if it would be dark by the time the next bus came. To make things more depressing, she could see Winsome Elementary rising above the homes in the distance.

"Hey, look, there's our school," said Byron cheerfully.

"Hurray," said Joy spiritlessly. But it was interesting to see the school all dark, without the familiar bluish glow of strip-lighting. It was kind of like coming across some terrible slumbering beast—it was hard to imagine the menace of its waking.

"So what's with that little weirdo from your class, with the bowl cut and the tie?" asked Joy.

"Oh, Morris," replied Byron wearily, chewing on a stick of licorice. "He's *gifted*. At least that's what Mrs. Whipple says. But it's not fair! He never has to do any work, just because she says he knows it all already!"

"Why don't they just skip him a few grades or something?"

"I don't know, I guess Mrs. Whipple doesn't want him to. Probably because she gets Morris to teach the class whenever she gets a call, which is a lot.

"And if you don't do exactly what he says when she's out of the room, Mrs. Whipple gives you a detention! He even made the whole class join some dumb club of his last week, making us all sign some paper before we could go out for recess."

"That sucks." Joy was stunned. Poor Byron! She thought she had it hard in Miss Keener's class. At least she didn't have any boy geniuses to deal with. Far from it.

"SPOOKY, SPOOKY, SPOOKY!"

Just then, a mass of soggy leaves landed heavily on Joy's head as Tyler went flying past on a bike, his snickering piggy-nosed cronies peddling their stumpy legs as fast as they could to keep up.

"She's scaring the leaves right off the trees!" he shouted. They tore off down a side street, laughing.

Byron dropped his licorice, gawping at the stagnant mess clinging to his sister's sunny blond hair as Joy stood there, stunned and silent. "Why didn't you do something, Joy?" he asked.

"Like what?" snapped Joy. It wasn't like she was Melody Huxley with a pair of silver-plated pistols or Dr. Ingram with a bottle of nitroglycerin. She was Joy Wells, harmless Spooky and figure of fun. Which was exactly why she'd wanted to stay out of stupid Darlington in the first place! Every step she took down here landed her in some new indignity. Couldn't anyone understand that?

But did it matter what anyone thought of her—or threw at her? They were losers, the Darling kids, and Tyler was Captain Ultradrip—the crowning accomplishment of his life being his ability to roof a tennis ball from the schoolyard.

But that was what was so maddening, Joy realized. They were losers under the lifelong impression they were winners! And why not? Everyone told them so. Parents, teachers, and coaches, all lining up to congratulate them on their looks, their athleticism, and their basic literacy. And they kept producing more of them. It was as if there was some factory spewing them out—a bunch of self-satisfied little robots whose only spark of creativity manifested itself in imagining new cruelties to inflict on those unlike them.

Joy looked at her reflection in the bus shelter glass. She saw a young Madame Portia staring back, hair speckled with leaves, and felt like crying. To everyone else, she was the loser, and always would be.

"Here comes another bus," muttered Byron, standing at the edge of the curb, unable to look at Joy as she picked through her hair. He turned his face away, letting the brisk wind spirit away a tear as the bus drew up.

❦ ❦ ❦

Phipps pulled into a parking spot outside the bus station. That was the worst job yet, he thought angrily. And thanks to an electrostatic charge lurking in his jester tights, the hairs on his legs were now standing uncomfortably on end.

What a pathetic operation. A case of chicken pox would have been a more authentic medieval experience, and arguably more fun, he thought, getting out of the car. The only thing he could imagine that could redress his humiliation at having served such an establishment was its complete and utter destruction. He made a mental note: Have the Misty Mermaid undercut Kiddy Kingdom by 50 percent on function rooms, with free sea-sponge cake to every party of fifteen or more. It was just what the plywood castle was crying out for: an extended siege.

In the meantime, he could take comfort in the fact that he wouldn't be asked back, having flatly refused to subject himself to "Pin the Tail on the Jester" like the usual stooge. There were limits. He had signed on as a wandering minstrel and that's exactly what they got—even if that meant wandering off. If a few fat-faced parents didn't like the fact that he wouldn't juggle, breathe fire, or grovel at the feet of some spoiled little brat, that was just tough.

He should sell the lute, he thought, and all the other

instruments while he was at it. He could get good money for them, and without any instruments he wouldn't be tempted to do these degrading gigs. So what if he was thrown out on the street? He could always sleep in his car—or move back in above the old shop.

Because the way things were going, he was going to wind up playing the harp at a New Age restaurant before long.

I'll hang myself with catgut first, he told himself.

He couldn't sell the instruments, he knew. He would just gamble the money away. Which would break his greatest rule: Don't touch his legacy. The legacy was everything, and his father's old instruments were the most valuable part, for now.

No, he had to hold on to them, along with the shop and its scrubby, windswept few acres. It was his future, if indeed he had one.

Phipps went inside the station and waited on the bubble-gum stained platform. A bus pulled in, making a wide turn and coming to a hissing stop between a pair of diagonal painted lines.

CITY EXPRESS, it said.

Phipps watched as passengers got their belongings down from the luggage racks and began disembarking. First off were a pair of young women with shopping bags. Then a few business men, and a mother carrying a newborn baby. Then an old couple, holding hands, careful not to fall down the steep stairs.

Finally a man got off, the shredded plaid lining of his leather jacket hanging down in strips, carrying a day bag and a guitar case plastered with stickers and gaffer tape. He rubbed his eyes and squinted up at the sun before fishing out a pair of sunglasses. Cheap plastic ones, Phipps noticed, that likely offered less UV protection than pressing a couple of beer bottles to your face. But what did it matter, when their owner had already fried every other major organ in his body.

"Vince," said Phipps, stepping forward.

"Octo! How's it going, man? Long time no see!" The man held out a tattooed hand.

"Too long."

They shook hands.

"Nice watch," said Vince. "And check out the threads," he added, looking up and down at Phipps's dark, pinstriped suit.

"What can I say? It comes with the territory."

"Well, it's quite the look you got going," replied Vince. "You must be doing all right, huh?"

"How was your trip?" asked Phipps, ignoring the question as they left the station.

"It sucked of course—I wouldn't exactly call that a tour bus, man. But I'm glad to get out of the big city for a bit. The chicks and the partying—it gets tiring, man."

"Well, you should find Darlington mercifully free of partying chicks," replied Phipps.

"So this is your hometown?" asked Vince incredulously. "I wouldn't have pictured you coming from somewhere so . . . regular."

"It's not exactly my hometown," replied Phipps. "I grew

up nearby, somewhere not quite so regular. They'd only just begun building this city then."

"Oh," said Vince, who didn't appear to be listening, but was instead looking at Phipps again. "Man, I can't get over you." He laughed, a little sneer creeping into his smile. "Next time you need me to play a gig, make sure to send a limousine, all right?"

Phipps was bemused. Play a gig?

Ah, that explains the guitar, thought Phipps—the clueless scumball thinks he's here to play a show. Phipps chuckled inwardly at the idea of it. After all these years, Vince still had no clue just how unremarkable a musician he was. And in the ego-driven fraternity of electric guitarists, Vince was the ultimate bottom-feeder—a bar-chord bozo. His solos—on the rare occasions he worked up the nerve to attempt one—sounded like a yowling cat at best.

Yet here he was, mocking Phipps with a curled lip. *Look at you in your suit—you sold out.* How predictable. Because for all his ripped jeans and eat-the-rich attitude, there was no bigger snob than Vince.

Phipps recalled his own years of living in a state of perpetual disgruntlement. He imagined himself in a safety-pinned T-shirt, his head a fleshy pincushion, his spiked hair the color of an eggplant. What a waste of time. But then again, it wasn't really his fault, growing up in such a backward community—a factory, pretty much, for spewing forth misfits and oddballs. Luckily, he had finally seen the error of his ways.

Now, thankfully, punk rock was dead—it was just a shame

no one had told Vince, a middle-aged man with his jeans rolled up over his combat boots. *We only let you in the band because you had a van, dirtbag. And even that didn't get us anywhere.*

"So what's the gig, Octo?" asked Vince. "Oh, and any possibility of getting something up front? I need cash bad."

"Yeah, bad news, man," said Phipps, slipping back into old manners of speech. "The show's been canceled—the vocalist got thrown in jail."

It sounded believable for something made up on the spot. Which reminded Phipps of another of Vince's musical failings: He couldn't improvise his way out of a paper bag.

"Huh? So I just spent eight hours on a bus for nothing?"

Vince sounded more like a little disappointed boy than an irritable lowlife whose leisure time was being wasted, Phipps thought contemptuously. "But wait, there's good news." He clapped a hand on Vince's shoulder. "I've got a little job to make up for it. Don't get me wrong—it's not like real work or anything. And it pays a lot better."

Vince made a face like he was chewing tinfoil. Phipps had to sweeten the deal quick or be left in the bus station huffing the fumes of a departing bus.

"With half the money up front," Phipps added.

Vince's face relaxed. It was his favorite tune—one of the few you could always count on him to play along to.

"So where'd the singer go?" asked Vince as they headed out of the station.

"Huh?"

"The vocalist—where'd he get locked up?"

"Oh. Anderson, I think," answered Phipps, hoping he

wouldn't have to provide a name. The secret to lying effectively was to never give too many details.

"Anderson," scoffed Vince. "That prison's practically a country club! Pilton is where they send the real deal—if he was in there, I could've put in a good word for him."

"I wouldn't have bothered," replied Phipps, adding: "He wasn't that great anyway. Once someone like that outlives their usefulness, I couldn't care less."

It was another secret of lying: drawing from the truth as often as possible.

Vince nodded knowingly. "Whoa, nice muscle car, Octo!"

Phipps bowed theatrically as he opened the door for him. Vince tossed his stuff in back and climbed in as Phipps made the long journey around the hood to the driver's side. Getting in, he glanced at the familiar tattoo on Vince's forearm: an ace of spades with "Live Hard" in blurry scrollwork underneath.

Phipps turned the key and the engine started up with a roar.

"Killer car!" said Vince as they pulled away.

CHAPTER 10

Mrs. Wells called up from the dining room. "Dinner!"
Joy was in the library, doing her homework, but
had passed out in the stuffed armchair by the glow of the
light-up globe. Outside, branches scraped against the leaded
windows as she'd sunk into a deep slumber, black and dream-
less, not even stirring when her math book slipped off her lap
and landed on the carpet with a thump.

It had been a very trying Monday.

"Dinner's on the table!"

Joy woke with a start. The wafting aroma of onions and
garlic was making her stomach growl. She pulled her wooly
cardigan tightly around herself and headed downstairs.

"There you are," said Mrs. Wells as Joy shuffled into the
dining room yawning. The rest of her family was already
seated before steaming bowls of stew. "Did you fall asleep,
sweetie? You looked so tired when you came home."

"School felt really long," Joy explained without elaborat-
ing. It had been a terrible day, and the last thing she wanted
was to crown it off with a half-hour lecture on coping
strategies from her mother. Tyler and his friends, embold-
ened by their leaf attack, had decided to devote their limited

attention spans to bombarding Joy with paper balls all day.

"Joy Wells," Miss Keener had finally shouted, "does this classroom look like a garbage can to you?"

"Pardon, Miss Keener?" Joy had replied, startled.

"The paper all around your desk—pick it up and put it in the wastepaper basket right away!"

Joy had begun to protest but quickly cut herself off. Why argue? Having to spell it out was only going to make everyone laugh even harder. And she could already hear Miss Keener's kittenlike purr as she gently scolded her little golden boys.

So, without a further word, Joy had collected up the balls as ordered. She then sat down again, chewing the end of her pen as if she couldn't care less. It had felt like a small victory—until thirty seconds later, that is, when another paper ball bounced off her back.

"Well, have a hot bath and get to bed nice and early then," said Mrs. Wells.

It was her mother's cure-all, passed down through generations. The sniffles? Bath and bed. The flu? Bath and bed. The plague? Bath and bed.

"You look exhausted too, Edward," said Mrs. Wells. "How was work?"

"Awful," he replied. "I spent the whole day arguing with a client who's refusing to pay his bill."

"How come?"

"Because he lost his case! He was appealing a rather staggering fine he'd received from FISPA for cutting down a tree on his property. It was his own fault—you can't just take a chainsaw to everything that happens to drip goop all over your sports car! There are regulations! The tree was a protected species!"

"Oh my," said Mrs. Wells. "You should have a nice hot bath and just get in bed, as well."

"Yes, yes, yes," said Mr. Wells, even though he only ever took showers. "Honestly, if I could do it all again, I think I would have gone into advertising."

Joy swallowed a mouthful of hot turnip.

"Dad, what's FISPA?"

"It's short for Federal Imperiled Species Protection Agency. They protect the environment from bozos like my client, and do a very good job of it."

"Do they protect creatures as well?" she asked.

"I would imagine so," answered Mr. Wells. "As long as the animals are part of the natural history of the area, that is. They don't take in stray pets or anything."

"Oh," said Joy, turning her attention back to her plate. With her parents always on the alert, it was important never to give away when she was seizing on an idea—especially when it was as red-hot as the piece of sweet potato she'd just inhaled.

One thing was for sure—the bog fiend wasn't anybody's pet.

🌸 🌸 🌸

Miss Keener was off sick the next day. The substitute teacher was a stout little man with thick glasses and a blazing temper. "I have zero appetite for nonsense!" he warned before handing out a stack of worksheets—and having meted out an incredible seven detentions the last time they'd met, the class didn't doubt him. The atmosphere remained about as lively as a morgue for the rest of the day.

Joy drummed impatiently on the seat in front of her as the bus made its way up the hill to Spooking. It was Tuesday, she reminded herself, and Tuesdays her mother taught a late class and her father usually had appointments. Sure enough, the driveway was empty as Joy and Byron were once again forced to leap from the moving bus.

"Byron, go up to the library and get started on your homework," ordered Joy as she unlocked the front door. "I'll make us a snack and be up in a minute." Byron kicked off his shoes and headed upstairs, dragging his school bag behind him. As soon as Joy heard the creak of the library door, she slipped into her father's office.

There, she picked up the phone and dialed 411.

She had been psyching herself up all day to speak to an operator but was instead surprised to hear a recorded voice asking her to listen carefully to the following options as they had recently changed. She waited and waited as each was carefully explained, glancing at the time on her father's desk clock. Finally, after enduring all seven options, she pressed number 1.

A robotic voice asked her to clearly speak the name of the person or business whose number she was seeking.

"The Federal Imperiled Species Protection Agency," she said in a deep voice like she imagined Melody Huxley might have had. She heard clicking noises.

"To call this number, say 'call this number,'" the robotic voice said.

"Call this number."

There were more clicking noises, and then it began ringing. Joy swallowed hard as someone answered.

"FISPAHOWMAYIHELPYOU?"

"Um, is that the Federal Imperiled Species Protection Agency?" asked Joy, unsure if she was talking to a human or a machine this time.

"YESITISHOWMAYIHELPYOU?"

Joy put on her Melody Huxley voice again. "I would like to report a new species of animal that might need protecting."

"WHATDISTRICTDOESTHISINQUIRYCONCERN?"

"Pardon?"

"WHEREISTHEANIMAL'SHABITATLOCATED?"

"Excuse me?"

"WHERE-ARE-YOU-CALLING-FROM?"

"Oh, sorry. Spooking."

"DISTRICTOFDARLINGTON. PLEASEHOLD."

Joy found herself unexpectedly listening to music. She looked at the clock nervously.

"Field Agent Wagner speaking," said a man, answering.

"Hello," Joy said.

"Hello. What can I do for you?"

"It's about Spooking Bog," she began to explain before realizing she'd forgotten to use her Melody Huxley voice. "I don't know if you are aware, but it's an amazing natural habitat," she continued huskily. "But now people are going to build some idiotic water park over it, with mermaids. And I was wondering if you could stop them."

"Ah yes, um, madame," said Field Agent Wagner. "I was

unhappy to hear we are losing another precious wetland, but I'm afraid there's nothing I can do. The agency has already reviewed the application. We raised a few considerations with the Darlington City Council and they agreed to accommodate them. So, other than that, there is nothing I can do, because the site is not an officially protected conservation area. But I do sympathize. Why not write a letter to City Hall? That's what I would do."

"What do you mean it is not officially protected?" asked Joy, dropping her Melody voice again. "But what about all the rare specimens? They'll be lost!"

"I'm afraid no protected species are under threat from the development—otherwise we would have put a stop to it. Is there something specific you are concerned about?"

"How about Ernesto?" asked Joy. "I mean, the huge snapping turtles that live there."

"Actually, that was one of our considerations," answered Field Agent Wagner. "And the City of Darlington has agreed to hire a reptile wrangler to capture the turtles and relocate the community. So that should put your mind at ease. Was there anything else? I'm afraid I'm terribly busy today. . . ."

Joy thought quickly. "Okay, but what about the plants?" she asked. "Like *Sarrencia illuminus*?"

The man coughed. "A lovely carnivore, which is a protected species—elsewhere, that is. The truth is that the electric pitcher plant is not native to the area. It was transplanted here about a hundred years ago to curb the populations of biting insects. Of course, it failed, and only succeeded in endangering a rather beautiful species of beetle.

"As a result, about ten years ago, FISPA started a campaign to wipe the plant out—we burned entire fields of them. So, if you say there are *Sarrencia illuminus* repopulating in Spooking Bog, I am a little cheered to think that some small good may come of this project."

Joy bit her lip. She was so angry with herself! Instead of helping to save the bog, she was actually making it worse! What did she know about this stuff? If only she knew as much as Madame Portia, or even better, Madame Portia's poor husband. He could have come up with a few endangered species in a second!

Which gave her an idea.

"Okay, maybe those aren't great examples. Have you heard of . . ." Joy paused, trying to remember the name Madame Portia had only dropped like thirty times during their visit. "Dr. Zweek?"

"Zweig? Dr. Ludwig Zweig?"

"Yes!" she cried.

"The name is somehow familiar," said Field Agent Wagner. There was the sound of rifling papers. "Could you refresh my memory?"

"He is an expert on Spooking Bog!" said Joy. "I mean, he was, before he died." Joy cleared her throat. "Anyway, Dr. Zweig said that he discovered something very important in the bog. A totally *new* species that no one knew about. And he was about to reveal everything to, er, scientific people, like you guys. But then he died, as I mentioned, which was bad timing."

"And what was it?"

"What was what?" asked Joy.

"The new species he found?"

There was silence on Joy's end.

"Hello?" asked the field agent.

"A flesh-eating fiend of incredible size!" declared Joy suddenly, quoting a line directly from E. A. Peugeot. *"Slumbering among the sphagnum since the dawn of time!"*

That had come out better than she'd expected. Even her Melody Huxley voice was right on the money. Joy smiled smugly to herself, then became aware of the complete silence on the other end of the phone.

"Hello?"

The man took a deep breath. "Umm, miss, madame, I'm not sure if this is some kind of . . ."

Joy looked up with fright—there was a figure looming in the doorway. It was Mr. Wells, holding plastic bags full of groceries.

"Joy, what on earth are you doing on the phone in my office?"

Striking with the blinding speed of a rattlesnake, she pressed the mute button. "No, I will *not* pass you to my parents!" said Joy sternly into the phone. "As I keep telling you, our family has a policy against telephone sales!" She hung up, sighing dramatically. "Oh, hi Daddy, you're home!"

"Will those people ever leave us alone?" asked Mr. Wells. "Good job, sweetheart."

✻ ✻ ✻

After Joy finished her homework, she played with Fizz for a while, who had been jumping at the sides of the terrarium desperately. He rolled over and over as Joy tickled his smooth stomach. Before long, he fell asleep on her lap with a giant grin.

That had been a close call in her father's office. But even if she was found out and punished later, it would still be worth it, she thought. The bog was part of Spooking's history, and she couldn't live with herself if she let it get swallowed up without a fight. How could her parents be mad at her for that? Still, it was probably a long-distance call and she'd been on for a while.

At dinner Joy was in a cheery mood. She was feeling triumphant. The Federal Imperiled Species Protection Agency didn't fool around, if her father's dealings with them were anything to go by. If there was something in the bog, they'd unearth it—and even get its face on a postage stamp in all likelihood.

Whether or not it would take kindly to either was another question, however.

"Joy?" asked Mrs. Wells, spotting the look of horror crossing her daughter's face. "Are you all right?"

"Huh?" asked Joy, snapping out of it. "Oh, I bit my tongue," she lied.

After helping out with the dishes, Joy went back up to her room. She got out *The Compleat and Collected Works* and opened the book to where it was marked in red silk ribbon.

She chomped the ends of her hair, reading. It was the climax of "The Bawl of the Bog Fiend," when the bad-tempered bacon baron leads a torch-wielding posse into the bog, hoping to flush out the unholy demon standing in the way of his piggish ambitions. And as expected, it didn't turn out happily, especially for the Prince of Pork, who wound up butchered like one of his hogs, his body parts raining down in a shower of chops on the fleeing survivors.

And though she'd previously tittered to herself over it, she now felt a less welcome sort of horror. Maybe calling in FISPA hadn't been such a great idea, she fretted. Wasn't Field Agent Wagner likely to meet a similar fate?

That would be awful. Field Agent Wagner, Joy guessed, was probably much like Dr. Ingram himself. Brave, inquisitive, ever calling "Hullo there!" into the black hole of the unknown.

Maybe she could just call him back and suggest he bring an assistant. . . .

There was a knock on her door.

"Come in," said Joy, startled.

"Sorry to disturb you," said Mrs. Wells. "I just wanted to talk about Halloween next week."

Halloween was Joy's favorite holiday, when Spooking was at the height of its powers. She loved rummaging through the cellar for some new costume, and then stalking the streets with Byron under an evil moon.

"What about it?"

Mrs. Wells took a deep breath, which was a sign for Joy to brace herself for bad news. Could Halloween be canceled or something?

"Byron was hoping to go trick-or-treating down in Darlington this year."

"Darlington?" shrieked Joy, outraged. "Why?"

"Well, I don't know if you've noticed, but the opportunities are somewhat limited up here."

"That's ridiculous—it's much, much scarier!"

"I'm not talking about that—I'm talking about going door to door getting candy. For example, how many homes in Spooking actually give out any?"

"Plenty," said Joy. She counted. "Six. Wait, seven if the Van Hurkles are back from abroad."

"The Van Hurkles? Didn't they give out those disgusting black things you said were like salted slugs?"

"They're a European delicacy, actually."

"You spat them on the carpet!"

Joy shrugged. "Well, I'm not from Europe."

"Anyway," said Mrs. Wells, changing the subject, "Byron heard at school that down in Darlington almost everyone gives out candy—the sweet kind. Not only that, a lot of people make a really big effort to decorate."

"Pfff." Joy was unmoved. Halloween in Darlington—what a ridiculous notion! It was like having Christmas in a volcano. Besides, their particular brand of horror was more of an everyday event.

"Joy, I thought you might not want to go," said Mrs. Wells sympathetically. "Especially after what happened on Sunday."

Joy blinked nervously. She had been careful not to mention getting ambushed by Tyler and his friends in Darlington. Her mother loved to "talk through" that kind of thing, which was often more painfully embarrassing than the actual event itself. She played dumb. "Sunday? The birthday party?"

"Byron told me that some boys threw leaves at you while you were waiting for the bus."

Joy could just see the incident as replayed in her mother's mind. The horrible sneers turning into cheeky grins, the mud-caked missile becoming something worth pressing in an album to preserve the wonderful seasonal memory. "I don't want to talk about it," said Joy. "Please?"

"But it's important, Joy. I think someone should explain how those things happen at this age, which is a very funny time for boys and girls. Remember, I was once almost twelve. And I was embarrassed by the sudden attention from boys, who tend to develop a bit slower than girls and do very silly things to impress whoever they have a crush on."

This particular misreading was more than Joy could stomach. She shuddered. "Mother, they do not have a crush on me, believe me," Joy said forcefully. "If they did, the next thing I'd want thrown at my head is a bowling ball."

"Joy Wells, why do you have to be so disturbingly graphic just to make a point?" asked her mother with frustration. "All I was trying to say is that I understand your feelings. And if you don't want to go trick-or-treating with Byron in Darlington, that's fine—I will take him around myself.

"I just thought maybe you'd enjoy a change of scenery and the opportunity to actually get some real candy for a change. But obviously I was wrong, as usual. . . ."

Joy watched her mother turn with a heavy sigh toward the door. She was a black belt in guilt trips!

Then something occurred to her. Halloween was the one time a year she could tramp around unsupervised at night without fear of grounding. It seemed a bit of a shame to waste it. For one, she had to speak to Madame Portia again, who was almost certainly hiding her knowledge about the bog creature. With FISPA possibly on their way, such information could very well save somebody's life. Not only that, she had to let Madame Portia know that Field Agent Wagner was on her side.

"Okay, maybe I could use a change of scenery," said Joy. "I'll do it. I'll take Byron trick-or-treating in Darlington if he wants to go that badly."

"Wonderful!" said Mrs. Wells, beaming.

"But I want to be picked up so we don't have to walk all the way back up."

"Of course!"

"We'll meet you at the bottom of the road up to Spooking Hill then," said Joy, "by the bog."

"What time?"

"Midnight?" said Joy.

"Try eight thirty," replied her mother. "Good night, sweetheart."

CHAPTER 11

Golden sunlight glinted off the steel and mirrored glass front of City Hall. Phipps passed purposefully through the automatic doors into the lobby. It was immense, made to look as if hewn from ancient sandstone, with tropical plants and a towering waterfall crashing from its apex. It was as if the architect was posing a rather clever question with the design, Phipps thought: What if the ancient Mayans hadn't vanished mysteriously with rare and remarkable dignity, but had instead become a sad race of civil servants? Of course, the plants were all plastic and the stone shaped from some sort of Styrofoam, but the piped-in animal cries were a nice touch, Phipps thought, smiling every time a visitor jumped in fright at the howler monkey.

Phipps rode the glass elevator past giant artificial parrots dangling from wires. The mayor's office was on the top floor, and had its own gym, sauna, lounge, and theater. Phipps's office was a floor below. It had no windows and faced a sea of gray cubicles, home to hostile city employees who glared at him as he passed.

"Mr. Phipps!" bellowed the mayor as the elevator doors opened. He was hanging around the pretty receptionist as usual, this time wearing a light blue, terry cloth sweat suit and smelling not unlike a particularly ripe grizzly bear. "You caught me on the way to the shower," the mayor explained, inhaling as if in superior need of oxygen. The receptionist giggled. "Just finished my morning run. No better way to start the day, I tell you."

"Yes, sir," agreed Phipps. He followed the mayor into the main office, trying his best not to breathe in the mayor's foul slipstream.

The office had a commanding view across Darlington. The mayor tossed his soaking work-out towel onto a chair in front of his broad mahogany desk—the very chair he himself usually occupied, Phipps noticed with disgust. "As a matter of fact," he continued, "I did get some exercise yesterday, hiking the length of Spooking Bog."

"How'd it go? Is the old woman packing up yet?"

"She's coming around to the idea," said Phipps with false optimism.

"I need better than that!" barked the mayor angrily. "I just took a call on speakerphone during my run—that's what they call multitasking, my man—and they say the dozers are ready to go. They can get in there as early as beginning of November. Remember, my investor friends aren't putting up a cent before the site's been cleared. Not a pretty little penny! And we can't keep floating this thing using the city's money. So I don't need sissy little assurances—I need a guarantee that goes *gong* when you slap it on the backside!"

Phipps clenched his jaw so hard, he thought he might spit a mouthful of broken molars right into the mayor's face. Instead he answered calmly: "She's packing up. Which reminds me, I made a few purchases—here are the receipts."

The mayor glanced at the slips. "Two wetsuits? A fourteen-volt reciprocating power saw?"

"A few items our animal handling contractor requested to complete his assignment," replied Phipps.

"Huh?"

"The reptile wrangler, sir."

"Pardon? It sounded like you just said *reptile wrangler.*"

"Mayor, we discussed this before."

"When?"

"A couple of weeks ago. We had a meeting while you were on the cross-training machine."

"The cross-trainer?" Mayor MacBrayne snorted. "You know I can't hear diddly on that thing, son!"

"Sir," said Phipps with a sigh, "in order to secure planning permission for the Misty Mermaid, we had to promise the Federal Imperiled Species Protection Agency that we would relocate some snapping turtles to another bog—"

"All right, more than I need to know," said the mayor, holding up a hand as he turned in his chair. "I just gotta keep an eye on the purse strings." There was a short whine as the huge paper shredder turned the receipts into confetti. "The best office is a paperless office. Did I ever tell you that, Phipps? Pay yourself back out of petty cash."

"Thank you, sir."

"Now, was there anything else? Because I have a date with a dollop of lavender shower gel and some essence-of-mint shampoo," said the mayor, dropping his sweatpants.

Phipps winced. It was the mayor's new method of terminating a meeting—sudden displays of unwarranted nudity.

"Good day, sir," said Phipps, his morning appetite ruined thanks to the mayor's luminous rear. With a curt nod to the receptionist, he got back on the elevator.

"Have a wonderful day!" called the receptionist cheerfully after him.

He returned to his office, where a lopsided pile of mail sat on his desk. One of his chief duties was to make sure that Mayor MacBrayne only reviewed correspondence requiring his immediate attention: complimentary sports tickets, free movie passes, or black-tie dinner invites. The rest Phipps was to delegate or destroy as he saw fit.

Stomach grumbling, Phipps opened the first piece, addressed with tight, childish letters.

> *Dear Mayor:*
>
> *I am writing with good news! A new group of concerned young citizens has come together who not only admire your tireless efforts at City Hall but share your vision of Darlington, City of the Future!*
>
> *We are called the Minors for Mayor MacBrayne—or the Triple M's for short. For an initial list of members, please see the attached signatures. Our numbers will only swell! Feel free to call on us to help re-elect Team MacBrayne if and when there is an election of any kind coming up. Is there an election of any kind coming up?*
>
> *Oh, it has also come to our attention that the location of the upcoming Misty Mermaid Water Park is Spooking Bog! The Triple M's applaud this great plan! Not only is this location serviced*

by the *Number 6 bus*, but getting rid of that swamp should help reduce Darlington's rather awful mosquito problem.

Respectfully,
Morris M. Mealey

Winner of the Darlington, City of the Future Contest
President / Treasurer / Speechwriter, Minors for Mayor MacBrayne

This Mealey kid was like a chafing rash, one that wasn't responding to over-the-counter creams. And were there any children in the city not privy to Phipps's plans for Spooking Bog?

Phipps balled the letter up and threw it out. He didn't have time for this, any of it. In a fury, he snatched up the remaining mail and hurled it into the wastebasket.

But the mention of the bog reminded him: He had to go see Vince. With any luck he hadn't strayed too far from the flea-bitten motel on the edge of town where Phipps had left him.

Because there was something else on the shopping list Phipps wanted Vince to pick up.

Something scary, for Halloween.

CHAPTER 12

After a hastily eaten supper of canned clam chowder, Joy and Byron began getting ready to head out for Halloween. Byron was dressing up as a knight despite Joy's trying to talk him out of it.

"I'm just surprised, that's all, after the beating you took at Kiddy Kingdom."

"Knights are cool," Byron had retorted grumpily. Plus, he thought, princesses liked them.

"What about something more original? Like a flesh-eating zombie dwarf? Or a moldy mummy from Pygmy Island!"

"Mom!" he'd shrieked. "Joy's making fun of my height again!"

Which was the end of the discussion. He looked good, though, Joy had to admit. The costume was made from an old wool sweater Mrs. Wells had spray-painted silver to look like surprisingly convincing chain mail. Then he wore a cape, a pair of rubber boots also sprayed silver, and a cardboard helmet and shield covered in tinfoil.

Byron's favorite part of the outfit, however, was the sword, which was the real deal. Steel with a leather scabbard, recovered among the forgotten personal effects in the basement.

It was a fairly short sword, but nonetheless barely cleared the ground once attached to Byron's belt.

Of course, the thought of Byron running around with it caused Mrs. Wells considerable alarm until they demonstrated how utterly dull the blade was. It had been intended for display rather than decapitation and disembowelment. Reluctantly, and with the order that Byron keep it in its scabbard at all times, his mother agreed to let him take it.

Joy, on the other hand, had opted for a less fussy costume. She had decided to go as 1930s adventure-woman Miss Melody Huxley, which essentially meant wearing her tweed adventuring outfit with her hair pinned up in an approximation of Melody's short flapper hairstyle. Joy would have happily left it at that, but she then remembered that she needed some sort of disguise to operate undetected among the Darlings. So she quickly painted her face a ghostly white and smeared black around her eyes until they looked more like gaping sockets.

"Melody Huxley," Joy announced to the mirror, "undead adventure-woman!" *Good enough*, she thought, slipping a heavy flashlight into her side bag.

"You two look so cute!" gushed Mrs. Wells as they came downstairs. "Stand together, I want to take your picture." She pointed a tiny digital camera at them as they stood with fixed smiles on the bottom stair. "Show your teeth, Byron! Better . . . Say cheese!"

Joy and Byron squinted at a pulsing red light before being blinded by a white-hot flash. They stumbled down uncertainly, unable to see anything except green splotches.

"Oh, look—so sweet!" said Mrs. Wells, showing the picture to her husband.

Mr. Wells opened the front door. "Here's a couple of pillowcases to carry your treats in," he said. "Your mother is going to drive you down. I'll stay home to give out candy in the unlikely event anyone comes by."

Indeed, the streets of Spooking were lifeless as they stepped out, and not a single trick-or-treater was anywhere in sight.

"It'll be a shame to miss all the fun up here," said Joy with a sigh.

"What fun, Joy?" asked Mrs. Wells, fetching the car keys from a hook near the door. "It's like a graveyard outside!"

"Exactly." What a great night she was going to miss, stalking the streets of Spooking under the dim amber streetlights. The houses cloaked in darkness and dripping with dread, daring her to ring their ominous doorbells. Then the delicious wait, wondering what shambling horror might answer. . . . She couldn't get enough of it.

Byron felt relieved. Joy always insisted on stopping at the most foreboding residences, where clearly no one had lived in fifty years or more. And not only was it terrifying, it was usually a complete waste of his trick-or-treating time. He wanted candy, great helpings of it.

"By the way, honey, I would watch your speed," said Mr. Wells. "There'll be a lot of excited kids out on the streets tonight."

"Of course, Edward," replied Mrs. Wells defensively. "I'm not such a menace, you know!"

"I wasn't saying you were—"

"I always drive carefully, dearest, Halloween or not. Because I don't think any night is a good night to hit a pedestrian, do you?"

"No, dear," answered Mr. Wells.

They climbed into the station wagon and belted themselves in. Mr. Wells waved from the porch as they slowly reversed down the drive before crawling down the street.

"Mom, this is ridiculous!" said Joy finally. "Halloween will be over before we even get there!"

"I don't want your father nagging me when I get back," explained Mrs. Wells. "Anyway, don't worry—I'll make up the time around the corner."

And so, as the lights of Darlington twinkled below, they hurtled down the crooked road. As they leveled off, Joy glimpsed the wooded perimeter of the bog, its spidery fingers flashing in the headlights. Beyond, its interior was an impenetrable blackness.

Back in a bit, she silently promised as her white painted lips turned up at the corners. She then spotted a curious sight—a black car, parked in the shadows by the side of the road.

At high speed, they passed a few strip malls and convenience stores before entering a residential section of Darlington. They roared past a sign: SUNNYVIEW STREET.

"Stop the car!" Byron cried. "STOP!"

Mrs. Wells slammed on the brakes.

"What is it, Byron?" she demanded, terrified. "Did we run someone over?"

"Um—I thought this looked like a good block," he answered, looking guiltily at his sister.

Joy simply agreed: "Yeah, this is far enough." She opened the passenger door. "C'mon, Byron, we don't have much time," urged Joy, looking at Melody Huxley's gold pocket watch, fastened to a buttonhole by a slim chain.

"You have plenty of time," assured Mrs. Wells. "I'll meet you at the bottom of the hill at eight thirty. Bye, kids! Be careful crossing the roads!"

Mrs. Wells pulled a U-turn, bumping up on the opposite curb before peeling out. Joy noticed a steady wind had picked up—some sort of storm was coming.

"Let's go," said Joy, glancing up at the branches flailing against the muddy evening sky. "By the way, I forgot to mention—I have a little errand I need to run before we meet up with Mom."

"Uh-huh," replied Byron, galloping ahead without listening. He'd actually made it to Sunnyview Street, home of the Primroses. The word around school was they had the best Halloween display in town, with their entire property transformed into one long terror-walk. Byron had been lost in a daydream for a week, imagining the possibility of a little strawberry-blond ghost leaping out to cocoon him in her sweet-scented sheet.

It had seemed like such a long shot that Joy would ever agree, and even if she did, that he would ever locate this particular street within the sprawling grid of Darlington. But here he was, like it was destiny.

But apparently it wasn't only the Primroses who made an effort. On every porch sat glowing pumpkins leering at them as spiders with pipe-cleaner legs crawled across giant synthetic webs. Cardboard headstones lined the lawns as hidden speakers howled and moaned and clanked.

"Like I'm so scared," remarked Joy. "Sunnyview Street—what the heck is the *view* supposed to be anyway? Your neighbor's garage?"

"It's called Sunnyview," replied Byron defensively, "because they mean it has a view of the sun."

"That's so stupid, Byron, it's probably true."

They went up to the door of the first dwelling they came to—which looked even more featureless and box-like up close, observed Joy—and rang the bell. A moment later someone dressed as a witch answered, wearing a grin so toothy and crazed that Joy shuddered to think they'd somehow stumbled across Miss Keener's house.

"Hello there, my pretties!" she cackled maniacally in an unfamiliar voice.

"Trick or treat," Joy said with relief. Byron stood mutely by.

"Oh, what great costumes!" enthused the witch. Unlike her counterparts up in Spooking, the householder apparently expected a verbal exchange before handing over any candy. "Let's see, you're obviously a brave knight. And you, young lady? What are you supposed to be?"

"Me? Just some dead old woman whose wardrobe I raided."

Horrified, the witch quickly dropped a big handful of candy into their bags.

"Happy Halloween!" called Joy as she headed down the stairs.

Darlington was definitely a busy place on Halloween night. Sunnyview Street was packed with trick-or-treaters.

Crowds rushed from door to door and bowled each other over as they took shortcuts across lawns. Among them were the usual vampires, ghosts, werewolves, and witches, but what struck Joy was how many were wearing the exact same costume: a black hooded cloak, a droopy-mouthed ghost-face mask, and blood-streaked plastic butcher knife—licensed properties, as her father would have said, from a recent movie featuring an unstoppable homicidal maniac. It was typical, Joy thought—even on Halloween they can't help dressing alike.

Byron hadn't noticed, however, as he tore up and down stairs, candy raining down on him in a deliciously sticky storm. After a night in Spooking, Byron could usually transfer his entire haul into the plastic happy-face mug on his desk, but down here, his bag was weighing him down after half a block! Shaking with excitement, he paused long enough to cram four toffees into his mouth. Then a flash of artificial lightning illuminated the next house, where jaunty lettering on a painted wooden mailbox spelled out a family name.

THE PRIMROSES

"Ow! What the heck?" protested a rotund little skeleton after a hard ball of brown toffee bounced off his head.

"Sorry!" sputtered Byron, choking.

The little skeleton stomped off.

Byron shivered as the ominous tones of a pipe organ began foreshadowing danger. Bloody figures swung above shadowy headstones rising up from a thick carpet of mist on the lawn. From somewhere indistinct came a disturbing babble of sinister voices.

This was it—the Primrose Halloween display. It was legendary at Winsome, with its trail of terror leading down into the dark satanic bowels of the usually welcoming home. And Byron had waited an eternity to see it.

Admiring the gruesome contrast of hanging, blood-stained bodies from an otherwise cheerful-looking cherry tree, Joy had to admit this place was pretty good. But it was starting to get late, she realized. She jogged after Byron, who was already elbowing his way through the crush of children on the front porch. From inside came sudden howls and terrified screams. Mounting the front steps, Joy saw a costumed group emerging from the garage, leading away a sobbing toddler.

"What, we're supposed to actually go *inside*?" demanded Joy with disbelief as she caught up with Byron. Stepping into a Darling's lair—now that was a horror she wasn't prepared for.

"Let's do this thing!" shouted a familiar voice behind her. She glanced over her shoulder as three kids in the droopy-mouthed maniac masks leaped up the steps, one of them landing in an action pose as if ready to plunge his plastic butcher's knife into some cheerleader's chest.

It was Tyler, she realized. Cringing, she turned quickly around.

"No stupid monsters better mess with me in there!" shouted Tyler, unleashing a flurry of knife work that sent Byron's cape flapping.

Byron turned with a glare—he wasn't in the mood to be backstabbed with a butcher's knife, plastic or not. In a few moments, he would be entering the home of Lucy Primrose!

"Did you see his face?" Tyler laughed. "Hahahahaha!"

"You better watch it, Tyler, or the little pipsqueak's gonna stick you with his sword!"

Byron turned with another black look. They burst out laughing again.

Joy dragged her brother forward. What was he doing? Now was not the time to get into something with these idiots. She had important business to attend to! Tangling with a bunch of Winsome cretins was only going to make them late.

Just then, Joy heard the unmistakable snip of a pair of scissors as the three maniacs began laughing hysterically. She quickly shoved Byron inside as the line surged forward.

They stumbled into a flickering strobe-lit hallway, their ears ringing as scary sound effects blared. As they followed the procession of children ahead, a hand suddenly shot out from behind a sofa chair, grabbing at them. Joy slapped it away impatiently as she read a sign above some stairs going down: THIS WAY TO YOUR DOOM.

"It says it's this way!" she yelled over the noise at Byron, who was locked in a hopeless struggle with the grabbing hand. Rolling her eyes, she yanked him free. "Downstairs!" she yelled in his ear. Looking back, she could see Tyler and his crew close behind them. She quickly headed downstairs after Byron.

The basement was bathed in black light and an ear-splitting loop of cackling noises was playing. An impenetrable fog of what Joy guessed was dry ice hung at waist level in the room.

"Where'd the other kids go?" asked Byron, alarmed. Joy shrugged, looking around for an exit.

Then the mist swirled and a lacquered coffin appeared for a moment in the center of the room, with a glow-in-the-dark sign pinned to the open lid:

HERE LIES YOUR CANDY . . . OR YOUR DOOM!

There was heavy thumping as Tyler and his friends came down the stairs. Whooping, they spread out into the fog, slashing the air with their butcher knives.

"Check it out!" Tyler shouted. "I found a real smoke machine!" A stream of white vapor shot over their heads as Tyler hefted the heavy piece of equipment to his shoulder.

"Crank that baby!" said one of the droopy-mouthed maniacs.

"Yeah!"

Tyler fiddled with the controls and a thick white plume gushed out, blinding Joy. There must be an exit, she thought desperately—the kids ahead of them couldn't have just vanished into thin air!

"Tyler, over here: a coffin! Smoke it, man!"

"Yeah, yeah, yeah!"

Then the heavy clouds parted. Something terrible sat bolt upright in the coffin: a skull-faced maggoty horror with blazing eyes.

"WHAT ARE YOU DOING?" it roared.

Tyler squealed. The smoke machine fell, hitting the floor with a thunderous bang. The basement walls resonated with a chorus of shrieks as the towering skull-faced creature climbed out of its coffin. The stairs shook as more children stumbled down into the thick soup, screaming hysterically.

A flailing arm connected with Joy's head. She staggered back, her hair falling down in a shower of bobby pins. "Byron!" she called out, spitting out a bitter hair-sprayed lock. Groping around blindly, she finally got a hold of someone.

But it wasn't Byron, she realized with horror as the face came looming through the fog. It was Tyler, crouching on the floor, his face streaming with tears.

"Help!" he pleaded, seizing the front of her tweed coat. Then his terrier face squinted at the face framed by two curtains of sunny blond hair. "Spooky?"

Someone suddenly switched on a light. The smoke turned a sickly yellow, with panicked children back-lit like circling black wraiths as the terrible skull-faced figure lurched at them.

Joy felt an unexpected rush of pleasure. Now this was what she called Halloween! She turned back to Tyler and twisted his finger until he released her coat with a sharp cry, then shoved him sprawling into the fog.

As she stepped back, something pulled her through a half-open door.

CHAPTER 13

S orry I punched you like that," said Joy, standing in the laundry room. Louden Primrose sat on the dryer pressing a damp cloth to his eye, which, if it felt anything like her knuckles, was probably pretty sore.

"That's all right," he answered with a laugh. "I was pretty much asking for it, grabbing you like that in the smoke. Nice costume, by the way."

"Thanks," said Joy. Louden wore a tight-fitting skeleton suit—with his face painted white and eye sockets black just like her, she noticed with a hot flash of embarrassment.

"I have to find my brother," said Joy. "We're not from around here, and he'll start freaking out if he can't find me."

"I would wait until my dad calms things down out there," advised Louden. On the other side of the door, they could hear the creature from the coffin evacuating children up the steps to the garage, the exit from the Primrose house of horror. "Your brother will be all right. He knows my sister Lucy, doesn't he, and she's around somewhere."

Joy nodded—it seemed impolite to get into an argument with someone sitting beside a pile of their own folded underwear. But she wasn't convinced. The last thing Byron would want would be to sit around making small talk with some girl from his class.

And she wasn't exactly comfortable being alone with Louden. He was looking at her with the same curious air he had worn at his sister's party, like she was an interesting museum exhibit or something.

"So you're from Spooking, right?" he asked.

Duh, thought Joy—as if the whole school didn't know that much. "Yeah," she answered coolly, wondering what offensive observation would follow.

"It must be pretty wicked up there on Halloween—why bother coming down to Darlington?"

"It was my brother's idea," explained Joy, surprised. "You can get more candy down here."

"Gotcha."

"But this place is pretty cool, actually. Your house, I mean."

"Yeah, my parents really go for it," replied Louden. "They love decorating for the holidays. Halloween, Christmas, Easter . . . It's one of their favorite hobbies."

"Ah," said Joy, suddenly considering how her parents didn't even have a single hobby, much less a favorite. And though Mr. Wells always made sure each year to erect a dangerously lopsided Christmas tree, Joy couldn't describe their halls as exactly decked.

A moment of awkward silence passed.

"So," Louden continued, "what do you think of Miss Keener?"

Miss Keener? Beloved teacher of sickly school-spirited suck-ups?

"She's okay," replied Joy diplomatically.

"Really?" exclaimed Louden. "I thought you'd totally hate her!"

"How come?"

"Well, for one, she picks on you a lot."

Joy blinked in surprise. "You think?"

"Sure. Keener plays favorites, and you're definitely not one of them."

Normally, Joy would have taken offense at this kind of blunt statement, but she sensed Louden wasn't saying it to be cruel. It was an obvious fact—one that she had noted herself on the very first day of school.

"Aren't you one of her favorites?" asked Joy.

"Oh, probably," agreed Louden with a laugh. "But that doesn't mean I don't think she's really annoying. Like having to say we feel great every morning?" Louden pretended to barf. "It feels like we are on some sort of stupid kiddy show or something."

"I know!"

"And not only that, she can be pretty mean sometimes. On purpose, as you know better than anyone," he added.

"What do you mean?"

"Like with your book report. I don't know why she didn't let you finish. Just because a few kids weren't listening? It was a lot more interesting than the rest of the crap everyone had done."

Joy couldn't help a smile from creeping over her face, with a glimmer of tooth in it. "Really?"

"Well, sure. Especially if it's true, like you say, that such a big important writer might actually have come from around here. Why not check into it at least? What's to lose? I mean, how many other famous people lived in Darlington?"

The smile vanished as Joy bristled. "E. A. Peugeot didn't live in *Darlington*," she corrected. "He lived in *Spooking*."

"I meant Spooking. Whatever. It's the same thing, really, isn't it?"

"No, it's not the same thing," said Joy, offended. "It's not the same thing at all!"

"Don't get all mad," said Louden defensively, slipping down off the dryer. "I just meant it like Spooking is Old Darlington or something."

"Old Darlington?" repeated Joy, incensed.

"I mean, like my parents take Lucy and me on trips to a lot of places with a really old section. It's usually the best part where everyone wants to go, where you can buy postcards and stuff. You know what I mean? Maybe Spooking will be like that one day if, say, someone proves that a famous writer like that Peugeot guy really lived up there. And how cool would that be?"

Joy had a vision of a line of idling buses blocking her view as crowds of camera-wielding tourists in short-shorts trampled her front lawn: "*Look, honey! Up in the window! A real live Spooky!*"

"No thanks," she replied bitterly.

Louden shifted on his feet uncomfortably. "Suit yourself. It was just an idea."

"Well, maybe you should keep your ideas to yourself," Joy shot back.

Louden went quiet. They stood in silence for a moment as he dabbed at his swelling eye. He finally announced: "It sounds like things are under control now, if you want to go find your brother . . ."

"Yes," said Joy flatly. She opened the laundry room door. Outside, the black light was now back on. Children approached the coffin with nervous giggles as the skull-faced monster sat up, moaning.

"It's just up those steps over there," said Louden, pointing.

"Thanks. I'm sorry about your eye."

"Don't worry about it. See ya, then."

"Bye," answered Joy. She marched past the coffin, not even looking as Louden's father offered her a little candy-filled bag with a black cat on it.

Joy hurried up the steps and out into the garage, looking for Byron. How long had she been in the laundry room?

"Joy!" called Byron crossly, jogging up the driveway. "Where were you? I was really worried!"

"Sorry, I got stuck inside—I couldn't find my way out with all the smoke."

"What do you mean? Kids have been coming out for, like, ten minutes!"

"Oh—I was also talking to someone. From school. And I figured you were probably hanging out with your friend Lucy."

Even in the dim light of the driveway she could see Byron's face change color, transforming him into what looked like some irate raspberry. "She's not my friend, she's just a girl in my class!" he snapped.

"Okay, sorry!"

They began walking, not even bothering to go up to the next house, but instead heading down the street in stony silence. Byron felt his temper cool. He was wracked by the dark specter of guilt, having lied to Joy again. He hadn't really been worried about her after all. The truth was, he hadn't even considered her whereabouts until just a minute ago.

He had been too busy blowing his big chance.

Blinded by a face full of dry ice, Byron had finally blundered out of the basement behind a stampede of shrieking children. He'd definitely missed something in there, he was sure, like where you were supposed to get the candy for starters. And what about Joy—did she get any? He'd stopped outside the garage to wait for her. Just then the three droopy-mouthed maniacs had stumbled out and run screaming up the driveway.

"Run, you big babies!" he'd shouted after them as loudly as possible without actually moving his lips or engaging his vocal chords. "Run!"

Down the street, he'd then glimpsed a heart-wrenching head of hair approaching.

It was Lucy.

She was dressed up as a fairy princess with a billowy gold dress and delicate-looking wings made of muslin stretched over wire. With her friends Ella and Kirsten on each side of her, she was struggling to both hold her wand and carry her heavy haul of candy.

Without a moment to lose, Byron had darted across the

lawn to intercept her on the path leading up to her house.

"Ah, Princess Lucy—how nice to see you," he'd pictured himself saying, arms folded with a finger held to his chin exactly like he'd seen on a magazine. "What an enchanting costume you are wearing. These? Oh, thank you, but they're just my work clothes. The sword? Yes, it is quite real . . ."

But instead he caught his foot on a cardboard headstone and disappeared into the artificial mist pumping across the Primroses' lawn.

"I've had enough," announced Byron. "I want to go home."

"Really?" asked Joy in surprise.

"Yes."

"Okay, if you say so," she said sympathetically. "Let's head back. But watch your pillowcase—you're dropping candy everywhere."

Byron groaned as he bent down to collect a few rockets and some packages of bubble gum from the sidewalk.

"The trouble is, we're a bit early to meet Mom," observed Joy as she drew out Melody Huxley's gold pocket watch. The hands were in fact now frozen on 6:32—it needed winding again apparently. "But wait—I just remembered there's something I need to do!"

"What?" asked Byron disinterestedly.

"I need to have a quick word with Madame Portia. So how about we just pop by before Mom arrives," she answered casually. "Call it one last trick-or-treat."

"The crazy lady in the bog?" shouted Byron, eyes wide in disbelief. "You want to ring her doorbell in the middle of the night?"

"Don't be silly, Byron," said Joy. "I'm sure she doesn't have a doorbell!"

"I'm not going! The bog is dark and scary and we'll get lost and drown!"

"But I brought a flashlight and we know the path now," Joy assured him. "It'll just take ten minutes, I promise."

"No way, Joy!"

"Okay, okay. But I'm going. Just wait for me by the road, then."

"Fine!"

"But I think I should warn you. Remember when I was telling you about the E. A. Peugeot story, and how the townspeople tried to make peace with the bog fiend by tying up hogs at the edge of the woods?"

"Yeah," answered Byron sulkily.

"Well, I'm just worried it might still come by once in a while to see if anyone left it a care package."

Joy felt bad at the sight of Byron's frightened face, but time was wasting—and with her pocket watch out of commission, she no longer knew how much.

"Personally, I think it's safer to come with me to see Madame Portia," she said reassuringly as he followed after her. "After all, she's lived in there for years and nothing's ever bothered her. The bog fiend probably likes her for whatever reason. So I'm sure it will leave us alone once it knows we're her friends."

Byron gulped. "But how will it know we're her friends?"

"Hmm, good point," said Joy, switching on the flashlight. "Let's run."

CHAPTER 14

My sword!" cried Byron miserably. "I lost my sword!"

It wasn't the only thing lost, thought Joy with panic as the flashlight beam lit up another glistening line of muddy hummocks. She was certain they should have come across Madame Portia's by now, but so far there was no sign of the submarine house. It was as if it had put down its periscope and dived.

The bog was impossibly dark, even darker than Spooking Cemetery on a moonless night. At least there the lights of Darlington always cast an inextinguishable glow. Here, nothing penetrated the heavy woods.

Then it began raining. Hard.

"Oh!" Byron stamped a rubber boot with an angry squelch. A side trip to the swamp wasn't part of a happy Halloween as far as he was concerned. Not only that, they'd figured out that Tyler and those jerks had snipped off the corner of his pillowcase and he'd been losing candy with each step ever since. The only things left were a few bags of chips that had been too big to go through the hole.

And now to top it off, his sword was gone.

"We're lost!" he shouted. "I told you this was a stupid idea, Joy!"

"Listen, we're not lost. It's just a little farther, honest," she replied, as much to reassure herself. They must be on the path, she was convinced—otherwise they would have surely drowned by now like Byron had predicted. Joy also thought they would come across Byron's sword on the way back; his candy, on the other hand, was a total write-off. Not wanting to be weighed down, Joy had stashed her own under an overhanging rock by the road. She'd give him half, she decided, when they got back. Which was still ten times what he'd have gotten up in Spooking.

That was, of course, assuming they lived.

Then, just as she was about to admit to Byron that it was time to prepare mentally for the possibility of dying from exposure, Joy spotted a series of windows, glowing like hot plates in the distance.

Madame Portia's portholes!

"See? I told you. There's her place over there."

Byron just grunted. They trudged across the deepening mud and clomped up the gangway, banging on the door with their fists.

"Go away!" screamed Madame Portia. "Be gone, devil, be gone!"

Joy realized she was probably unused to visitors pounding on her door on a stormy night. "Hello, Madame Portia!" she called cheerfully above the howling wind. "It's Joy and Byron Wells."

A heavy bolt slid back and the door swung open.

"Children!" cried Madame Portia. "Have you lost your little minds? What are you doing out here in the middle of the night? Get inside, quick, QUICK!" She slammed the door shut and quickly bolted it behind them.

Joy and Byron stood shivering. While it was some comfort to be out of the rain, the orange light spilling from Madame Portia's parlor had turned out to be somewhat misleading. It was cold and damp inside and smelled worse than last time. And the rats, having plainly made themselves even more at home, were now leaping across the tops of her furniture.

"Again, what is the meaning of this?" demanded Madame Portia. "Your parents will be frantic with worry! My stars—I can only hope one of them isn't a lawyer!"

Joy gave Byron a sideways glance, but he wasn't paying attention. Instead, he was perched on the edge of a moldy sofa chair, hugging himself. "We're sorry for disturbing you so late," she replied brightly. "But our parents aren't worried about us. It's Halloween and we're out trick-or-treating!"

"Ah," said Madame Portia. "That explains why your brother is wearing aluminum foil." She turned to frown at Joy, whose blackened eye sockets were now streaming down her face. "Your costume, however, I don't quite get. Anyway, I have no candies or even cookies left, children, since you ate me out of house and home last time. But you should know it's very dangerous to venture into the bog at night!"

"We know, Madame Portia, that's why we're here. Spooking Bog itself is in terrible danger and we need your help to save it."

"My help?"

"Did you know that they are planning to build a water park here? With mermaids?"

Madame Portia stared at Joy incredulously. "The City of Darlington has been trying to get us out of here for a while, for sure. But a water park? I can't believe it!" cried Madame Portia, pinching her face in disgust as she began pacing. "And what is a water park exactly?" she asked absently.

"It's a type of amusement park. You know, where you slide down those giant tubes."

"Oh, yes . . . ," said Madame Portia, again checking that the door lock was secure. "Whatever—they can build a trailer park for all I care, because I'm getting out of here!"

It was then that Joy noticed that Madame Portia was now brandishing a golf club, and it seemed an unlikely night to be practicing her chip shots.

"Madame Portia, what's wrong? Are you frightened?"

"Am I frightened?" she repeated with a snort. "Like you don't know!"

"Pardon?" asked Joy.

"You're the one who insisted I read that awful story! With that horrible monster that stalks the night! Of course I am frightened—of being ripped limb from limb!"

"'The Bawl of the Bog Fiend'? By E. A. Peugeot?"

"Yes. And it's out there, all right!" Her voice dropped to a whisper. "I've heard its squealing howl, you know, just like it was written. Three nights in a row it's been coming for me, sniffing at my doorstep. When I heard you knocking just now, I thought it was the creature, trying to break in to eat me!"

"Madame Portia, calm down," said Joy reassuringly. "It's just a story, that's all." Byron's eyebrows fell like a dark avalanche as he glowered at her. The old woman wasn't listening, however. She was peering out a porthole, muttering some sort of prayer in another language.

"Madame Portia!" Joy shouted. "It's all made up! There is no such thing as the bog fiend!"

Joy couldn't believe her own words.

She might have long blown off Santa Claus, the Tooth Fairy, and the Easter Bunny as wishful thinking, but this was the bog fiend she was talking about, the yellow-eyed monster that terrorized an entire town, exploding from the bushes like a tooth-covered freight train! Could she really think for a second there was no such thing?

Just then, they heard it. A terrific crash outside followed by a dreadful squealing sound, as if made by some diabolical piglet.

"Here it comes again!" shrieked Madame Portia, tearing across the room. The golf club clattered to the floor. With a remarkable display of strength, she wedged a heavy oak chest of drawers against the front door. "I hope that holds! Or we're all doomed! Doomed!"

Joy ran over to the nearest porthole. Byron, having shaken off his initial paralyzing horror, was now entering full-on panic mode and desperately trying to drag a sofa chair twice his size toward the entrance.

There came another squeal, much closer this time. It reminded Joy of one of her father's old tools—the one he sawed open his finger with, thus permanently ending his enthusiasm for carpentry in a single ragged, blood-spurting gash.

"That's it!" howled Madame Portia. "We're all going to die!"

"Die?" protested Byron. "But you said we would live to be a hundred."

"Oh, that doesn't mean anything," shot back the old woman irritably. "No one's life line ever stopped them from stepping in front of a bus. It's called a *guesstimate*, assuming you eat sensibly and exercise. But it's too late for that now! Oh my, oh my!"

"We have to stay calm," ordered Joy. She tried peeking out of the porthole again. The only thing she could see was Madame Portia, clutching a macramé pillow and trembling on a chaise lounge behind her, reflected in the glass. "Turn out the lights!" The reflection of Madame Portia shook its head violently. "Whatever it is can see in, but we can't see out," Joy added impatiently.

This particular observation put Byron into immediate motion, and within seconds he'd wiped out every lamp with the golf club, plunging them into complete darkness.

Joy peered out again. This time she could see the faint outlines of trees and the black surface of the dismal little lake surrounding them. Nothing moved. She held her breath, trying to listen above Madame Portia's unrelenting moans.

"Shhhh," she said finally.

There was a shower of glass as the porthole to her immediate left exploded inward. Joy hit the deck as Madame Portia screamed. There was splashing outside, then suddenly the walls resounded with a terrible impact. Then the horrible squealing again, right below them.

There was a terrifying crack and the whole house shook. And then another.

"It's destroying the stilts!" shrieked Madame Portia. "Oh no! It wants to bring us down so it can open us up like a canned ham!"

There was another crack, and the front of the structure fell down with a huge splash.

Everyone was thrown to the ground. Everywhere, furniture and books rained down with thunderous bangs. Joy heard a heavy sideboard sliding toward her. She ducked blindly just as it went over her, clipping her arm with a terrible jolt of pain. All around came tremendous crashing sounds.

At last the noise stopped. Almost immediately, Joy heard the silence broken by Madame Portia, moaning softly.

"Byron, are you okay?" she called out into the darkness.

As the front of the house pitched forward, Byron had slid down the floor, coming to a stop under a dining table where he had borne the full force of the rat evacuation, rushing over him like some furry river. His mind clung to its last shred of sanity: a vision of cheerful pumpkins with fiery eyes and the sound of individually wrapped treats landing softly in his pillowcase. A last squeaking rat used his belly as a trampoline.

"No," replied Byron.

Joy tried to think of some comforting words for him. Making light of almost certain death—wasn't that what big sisters were for?

"It'll be all right," she whispered. "I think it's gone."

At that moment, there came another blast of hideous squealing as the back stilts began cracking one by one. Inside, they screamed as the other end of the house fell with an almighty splash.

Then, before anyone could recover their senses, the house began moving again, sideways.

"We're rolling over into the pond!" cried out Madame Portia in horror. "Someone help us! Someone save us!"

Madame Portia's worldly belongings were turned upside down, crashing together, splintering and smashing and shattering as if run through the destroy cycle of some demonic tumble dryer. Joy somehow caught Byron and held him tight as they were tossed among books and broken furniture. After what seemed like an eternity, they finally came to a rocking halt, lying painfully amid the debris.

Joy staggered unsteadily to her feet, still holding on to Byron. Droplets of water hit her face. She looked up and saw the scuba tube Madame Portia had pointed out, now a twisted, gaping hole with its bent ladder leading out to the dim world above.

They had rolled completely upside down.

Icy black bog water began rushing in.

"We're sinking!" cried Byron.

"Come on!" shouted Joy. She clambered onto a pile of splintered wood and stuffing. "Byron, grab the ladder," she ordered. Groaning with effort, she shoved him up into the gloom. "Madame Portia, where are you?" she called into the darkness. "Madame Portia!"

There was no reply.

From her perch on the broken furniture, Joy suddenly felt the water rush around her ankles. She leaped for the ladder as the water surged beneath her, carrying her upward out of the hatch where Byron clung desperately to the slimy underside of the house.

"Byron, jump!" she yelled, grabbing his hand. They jumped, landing hard on the broken gangway and then scrambling to shore. Panting in the mud, Joy and Byron watched in horror as the house sunk under the pond.

Poor Madame Portia! Joy's only hope was that she'd been knocked unconscious and was at that instant dying in peaceful oblivion. She felt like crying, but then realized something was still out there, something terrible, and it wouldn't be long before it smelled the sharp scent of flesh on the wind. Her left arm ached and no longer bent properly. They had to get moving! Joy felt for her trusty leather side bag, thankfully still hanging at her hip.

"Turn off the flashlight, Joy," Byron whispered.

"But we need to find the path—and according to Peugeot, the fiend doesn't like bright lights."

"Turn up the flashlight, Joy."

They quickly got to their feet. But where was the path? With the house gone, Joy had completely lost her bearings. Byron stood frozen with panic as Joy swept the woods with a trembling beam, illuminating a ghostly tangle of branches in every direction. It all looked the same to them. Then the light caught something hideous—glistening black with luminous yellow stripes and a terrifying tusked face. The children screamed as its bright eyes fixed on them.

"Run, Byron!" shouted Joy.

The two children bolted for it as Joy pointed the flashlight behind them in the hopes of dazzling the creature. Desperately they scrambled through the undergrowth, falling in the muck as they ran for their lives. Hearts pounding, they tore through the bog until they finally collapsed, lungs burning.

"I can't run anymore," sobbed Byron. "We'll never get out of here!"

From somewhere behind them, a shrill cry reverberated, unmistakable in its frustration and rage.

Joy hugged Byron. Wide-eyed, she pointed the flashlight up ahead. Nothing had changed—everything looked the same, brown and featureless. She moaned as a fresh wave of pain radiated up her arm as she held him.

"What's wrong, Joy?" Byron sounded alarmed.

"It's nothing," she lied, biting her lip as another spasm wracked her. She blinked away tears. Then, a short distance away, she spotted something colorful. "Look, over there—it's a pack of Super Sours!" she shouted with relief. "Come on, Byron! It's your candy trail. We just have to follow it out."

The children leaped to their feet, hope giving them renewed energy. They sprinted over to the pack of Super Sours as Joy began sweeping the muddy horizon with her flashlight.

"There! A pack of licorice!" cried Byron. "And my sword!" he shouted, pulling his beloved weapon from the mud.

"Keep going—there's bubble gum up that hill!" shouted Joy.

And so they raced along the trail of rockets, lollipops, and miniature chocolate bars. At last, they burst through a wall of face-whipping saplings and landed on the road.

A car screeched to a halt in front of them. There was a whir as the passenger window rolled down. "Joy, Byron!" called Mrs. Wells. "Get in the car this instant!" The children tore open the door and flung themselves inside.

"Step on it, Dad!" shouted Joy. "Go! Go! Go!"

At Joy's command, Mr. Wells began executing a painful three-point turn like a sixteen-year-old with a nervous condition taking his driving test for the first time. Joy exhaled in frustration. It was typical: The one time they would have actually been made safer having their mother at the wheel, she was shotgun. "Hurry up, get us out of here!" Joy shrieked at the back of her father's head.

"That is enough, young lady!" shouted Mrs. Wells in her high-pitched voice, signaling that she had hit the cathedral ceiling of parental outrage. "Look at the state of you both—you look like you've been rolling in mud!"

Joy looked back nervously through the rear window as Mr. Wells slowly drove up the hill. They were in the clear, she finally decided.

"Look at me when I am speaking to you, Joy!" blasted Mrs. Wells. "Where were you? And don't tell me you went back into those woods again!"

Joy didn't enjoy fibbing to her parents, especially in front of Byron, but what was she going to tell them? That some witchy old woman they'd befriended had just sunk to the bottom of a black lake before their eyes? Or that they'd narrowly avoided being eaten by the bog fiend, a creature straight out of the book her mother disapproved of? Which proved it was all true, by the way—that Spooking really was the terrible town chronicled by E. A. Peugeot?

Now there was a recipe for a grounding—just heat and serve.

Joy would have to reason with Byron later. He was completely mute at this point anyway. She squeezed his hand gently before adopting a new strategy: going on the attack.

"Where the heck were you guys?" Joy shrieked. "We had to go into the woods to get out of the rain. We could have died of exposure!"

Joy felt Byron's hand tremble.

"We were waiting at the foot of the hill, Joy," replied Mrs. Wells defensively, turning in her seat again. "Right where we arranged."

"And where's all your candy, kids?" asked Mr. Wells.

"Gone," said Byron bitterly, breaking his silence. "It's all gone."

few last obscene-sounding gurgles broke the surface of the pond. Then the old woman's house was gone. Phipps lay in the mud twitching as Vince staggered around above him.

"I'm serious, Octo," Vince insisted. "I'm, like, blind, man!"

"You are not blind," Phipps snapped impatiently. He struggled to pull off his ski mask with one hand as his mud-caked left arm swung uselessly. "It was just a flashlight—you're dazzled, that's all."

"Nah, nah—it was one of those new super-bright LED ones or something, the kind they warn you not to point at anyone's face. I could have permanent vision damage here, man."

"Well, at least you didn't have a house roll over you!" exploded Phipps, whose arm happened to be in the path of Madame Portia's home as it had become unexpectedly mobile. Thankfully, the soft deep muck had saved the limb from being crushed into pink paste. However, it was now most certainly broken if the white-hot agony and snapping sound were anything to go by. All thanks to the ham-fisted

Vince, whose handling of a power saw had proved no more competent than his handling of a guitar.

"And what about the kids?" shouted Vince, throwing down a horrible-looking rubber Halloween mask—the snarling face of a hideously tusked boar. "You never said anything about kids being in there!"

Phipps didn't answer. He had seen them too—a blond girl and a dark-haired boy, leaping clear of the twisted gangway just before the house slipped into the depths of the pond. Even more strangely, they had looked somehow familiar. Who were they? And what were they doing there? And most importantly, what had they seen? It was weighing on his mind almost more than his throbbing limb.

"And the old broad is definitely dead, you know," lectured Vince, the yellow striped sides of his black wetsuit glowing in the dim light. His sight had apparently returned as he strode up and pointed a finger directly at Phipps. "You killed somebody, Octo. Just so you know."

"*I* killed somebody?" protested Phipps. "You were the moron holding the power saw!"

Without warning, Vince kicked Phipps hard in the stomach.

"Hey, you said to make the house uninhabitable!" bellowed Vince, hovering menacingly over Phipps as he writhed in pain. "Can anyone live in that house now? Can they? No. Which means my job was done. Whoever was in there at the time was *your responsibility.*"

Phipps tried to get to his feet but doubled over retching.

"It's just like back when we were in the Tongs," continued Vince, pacing back and forth like an agitated bull. "It's always everybody else's fault according to you. Well, I'm not in your idiotic band anymore, so let me tell you: That crap is getting real old."

So this was how it was going to go, thought Phipps wearily. Of course—Vince was like an animal, but the most pathetic sort of predator, only able to pick off prey when it was injured or separated from the herd. And now that Phipps was both, Vince's fangs were finally showing. Phipps watched nervously as Vince picked up the portable saw and began admiring the vicious-looking blade that had sliced through the thick stilts of Madame Portia's house as if they were mere sticks of pastrami.

"What a complete waste of time, that band," muttered Vince. "You know, we only stuck around because you said we'd get a record contract. But nothing, ever, except more promises." Vince chuckled to himself. "I still can't believe how long we bought it all. What were we, a bunch of morons?"

Phipps decided not to field such an easy question, not with Vince hulking over him with a dangerous power tool. Instead he continued glaring up at Vince from the ground, remembering how his bandmates had always conveniently cast themselves as victims rather than the masters of their own misfortune.

Phipps recalled the events contributing to the band's ultimate failure very differently.

Like that stifling hot summer's night at a music festival in the city, when a record producer had flown in from overseas to check them out. The festival was set in a huge tent on some glass-strewn parking lot lined with portable toilets. It was packed to capacity, an uneasy mix of subcultures colliding violently as a procession of noisy bands blared above them.

The Black Tongs had finally been up, swaggering on stage with uncommon menace. The crowd fell into an eerie silence. Amid the sounds of lazy cymbal crashes and popping guitar leads, Phipps had taken the center, a dented trumpet under one arm and an electrified lute under the other. Squinting at the red-hot stage lights, he'd counted off: One, two three . . .

"And this is just like another one of your crappy gigs," spat Vince, startling Phipps from his recollection. "Another dirty hellhole you've dragged me into! But don't say it, you're right: At least this time, I don't have to drag my three-hundred-watt amp up four flights of stairs. And at least this time, I'm actually getting paid for once. On that note, I probably should mention that you now owe me double."

"We had an agreement!" shouted Phipps, outraged. The words were hardly out of his mouth before Vince kicked him again, this time square in the chest. Phipps wheezed horribly as the wind was knocked out of him.

"Well, I'm reopening the negotiations," said Vince. "Chew this deal over: You pay me double like I said and I'll agree not to boot you again. How about that—sound fair? And as a bonus, I'll throw in forgetting this whole business about sinking the little old lady."

"You don't understand," croaked Phipps. "I can't pay it—I can't even pay my own rent right now."

"Not cool," replied Vince darkly. "Okay then, what else do you got? Let's see. Hey, I've been thinking—I'm really not so hot anymore on this whole taking-the-bus business. . . ."

Phipps looked back at Vince blankly before a look of horror passed over his face. "No!" he shouted. "No way!"

"Octo, Octo, Octo—don't be like that. A guy my size needs a big ride."

"You can't have my car!" screamed Phipps.

"C'mon, I'm trying to do you a favor here. If you're so poor, do you really need an old gas-guzzler like that hanging around your neck? Plus, let's face it—you do look a bit stupid, driving a macho machine like that around in that wimpy little suit of yours. Besides, look around you—this is minivan country you're in, my man."

"Go to hell!" Phipps told him.

"Tsk, tsk, tsk," said Vince, holding the saw up. "Then you and me have a problem." The blade suddenly sprang to life with an angry buzz, inching toward Phipps's face.

"All right!" cried Phipps over the noise. For all his faults, Vince always excelled as a thug—it was his one true talent. "All right, I said."

The blade ground to a halt inches from his eye.

"The keys."

Phipps struggled to unzip the pocket of his wetsuit with a shaking hand. He threw the keys at Vince, who snatched them greedily out of the air.

"Nice." Vince laughed, examining the squishy fake eyeball on the end of the keychain. "You're a sick puppy—but that's what I always liked about you."

Phipps stared hatefully as Vince pocketed the keys.

"Thanks. Now to show my good faith, I'll return the favor." Vince tossed the saw high over the pond.

Phipps watched in horror as it landed with a splash. "What do you think you're doing?"

"Man, you make a lousy criminal. It's called getting rid of evidence—also known as covering up your crime," explained Vince. "Don't worry, it's all part of our new agreement, so you don't have to thank me."

"You can't leave the saw here at the scene, Vincent! Our fingerprints are all over it!"

"Oh yeah. Maybe that wasn't such a great idea," Vince admitted. "Don't worry—I'll get it back," he promised, wading into the pond.

Phipps couldn't decide which was worse—his broken arm, his forfeited car, or this final display of staggering stupidity. Together, they had become simply unbearable. Phipps screamed, a long shrill note of despair. Breathless, he then blacked out.

Phipps awoke sputtering and coughing a few minutes later, his lungs burning with foul miasmic fumes. Ooze caked his face and mouth. He retched and spat.

There was a splash nearby. Phipps looked up and saw Vince's dim outline rising up from the black surface of the water. The moron was nowhere even near it, thought Phipps as Vince dove under. Phipps watched, a glimmer of a smile cracking his face. He was in remarkably less pain now, he realized, climbing unsteadily to his feet. In fact, it suddenly all seemed kind of funny somehow.

"Yeah, right over there," called Phipps. "You're getting warmer. Warmer. Warmer . . ." He pictured with delight the hungry leeches latching onto Vince's face at that moment.

"Colder! Colder! Colder!" Phipps stumbled into the pond after him, laughing uncontrollably as he fished around the shallows with his working arm.

Then he remembered—the festival, the time that record producer had flown in to see them, the Black Tongs, live and onstage. Even twenty-five years later, the memory was just as vivid, but never had it seemed so funny: Vince, out of tune and out of time, knocking a beer into his amplifier and giving himself an electric shock as the guy from the record company wandered off toward the lesser stink of the portable toilets.

Tears of mirth blinded Phipps as he raked his fingers through the sludgy matter of the disgusting pond floor. Something jagged tore open his index finger. It was the saw, right where he thought it was! He hefted the power tool awkwardly with one hand. It looked in a terrible state, dripping and covered in filth. He pressed the trigger and it came to life, spattering mud into his snickering face. It worked! What an amazing device, he marveled, completely dependable, merciless, never questioning its purpose in its master's hand. What a rare and precious thing to just throw away like that!

Just then, Vince broke the surface, face covered in leeches. Phipps laughed so hard, he was barely able to breathe.

"Something just brushed up against me!" screamed Vince, coughing up pond water. "There's something in here!" he shouted, thrashing madly toward Phipps. "It's not funny, man!"

And for once, Vince nailed the exact right note—it really wasn't funny anymore.

CHAPTER 16

A fresh white cast pinned Joy's notebook to her desk. She sat, pen poised, staring at the empty lines as the rest of the class dutifully copied from the blackboard.

Yesterday Joy had woken up from a fitful sleep to realize that there was definitely something seriously wrong with her arm. Unable to get dressed, she had come down to breakfast in her pajamas and reluctantly shown the swollen limb to her parents. Horrified, they had taken her straight to Darlington General. A few X-rays later, they had determined that her arm was fractured in two places.

"That's two broken arms this shift—a regular epidemic," the doctor had said, yawning. "The other guy slipped on some candy and fell downstairs. What's your story, little miss?" he asked Joy with a wink.

Without bringing up the destruction of submarine-like houses by primordial horrors, Joy had been at a loss to explain. So she hadn't even bothered trying, and instead stared blankly into space. It was the same technique she'd used when her parents had questioned her earlier.

"The young lady appears to be suffering from mild shock," the doctor had informed her parents. "It's pretty common. My best guess is she probably ran into a tree or something. Kids get excited on Halloween and don't look where they're going—just be thankful it wasn't a car she ran in front of. Anyway, her arm should be perfectly fine in a few weeks. And she can head back to school as soon as she feels up to it—even tomorrow if she wants."

Lightheaded from painkillers, Joy had almost confessed that her cast would probably crumble into dust long before she'd ever feel up to heading back to Winsome, but thought better of it. The more she kept conversation to a minimum, the less explaining her mother would keep insisting she do. Besides, there was no way her parents would let her stay off another day now, not after the doctor's cheerful prognosis.

After the Wells family had returned home, Joy had slept away the remainder of the day. It had been a troubled slumber. She had dreamed of running through a shadowy forest, its muddy floors full of staring eyeballs that popped loudly with each footfall. Then of being trapped in a metal tube rolling around on the bottom of a terrible sea as she screamed and pounded on its walls.

Joy had woken up the next morning with a start.

"Sorry for waking you, my dear, but we need you to go to school today," Mrs. Wells had said softly, standing at her bedside. "Your father and I missed a lot of important work yesterday, and as the doctor said, the sooner you go back, the better."

Joy had known there was no point in offering her clear recollection of the doctor's exact words in argument—she was going to school, like it or not. Instead she had stood wordlessly as her mother helped dress her. In the kitchen she had fully intended to ignore any questions about her well-being, but no such inquiry ever came. Her parents had expressed their concern otherwise: with a round of sighs and an extra-special breakfast of frozen blueberry waffles heated in the toaster.

Joy had then marched out with Byron to meet the bus, which had delivered them to school. Joy now sat quietly at her old desk, feeling like an unmanned ship whose crew was washed overboard in a violent storm—an empty vessel, adrift, her course only determined by the pitching of the sea.

Upon seeing her injured arm, the other children had extended the greatest kindness they were capable of—pretending she didn't exist. Relieved, Joy thought back to a memory of her mother, sitting in front of the fireplace with an intriguing-looking book.

"What are you reading?" Joy had asked.

"It's called *The Lonely Gunman of Solipsism*," Mrs. Wells had answered, marking her place with a slender finger. "It's a new course book I'm evaluating. My students think it's *hip*," she'd added, as if having no idea what the word meant, before pushing away a strand of unfathomably dark hair that had become hooked on her glasses.

"What's it about?" Joy had asked.

"Oh, it's just an old theory of philosophy, really," Mrs. Wells had said. "That nothing really exists other than yourself."

Joy had become even more curious. "What does that mean?"

"Well, for instance, you know you are Joy Wells. And you

know I am Joy Wells's mother. And you can see the orangey red flames in the fireplace and smell the smoke.

"But how do you know that I see those same flames? Or smell the smoke? Or see or smell anything for that matter?"

"I don't understand . . ."

"Well, am I even a real person at all? Maybe you are the only thing that really exists, and I am just a figment of your imagination, saying and doing all the things that your sub-conscious mind believes I should, being your mother."

Joy had thought the possibility over. "Could that be true?" she had asked, alarmed.

"It can't be proven, but it can't be disproved either, so it's a possibility. In theory." Mrs. Wells opened the book and read a passage aloud: *"The only true reality then, is made up of the changes experienced by the self, as the self can know nothing for sure but its own modification. Which suggests the possibility that nothing exists outside of the self, and reality is the sum of the self's imaginings."*

The possibility that nothing was real except her own imagination had been a strangely cheering notion. But then what about the rest of her family? Did that mean they didn't really exist?

"Do you believe it?" she had asked her mother. "I mean, do you believe that *you're* the only one who exists?"

Mrs. Wells had laughed. "Are you just a figment of my imagination, Joy?"

"No," she answered finally. "I guess."

"Then of course I don't believe it," said Mrs. Wells. "Because you wouldn't lie to your mother about a thing like that." Mrs. Wells caressed her daughter's slim shoulder. "It's all just a silly game, Joy, and an easy way for my students to get out of answering more important questions. I wouldn't dwell on it."

But advising Joy not to dwell on such a topic was a bit like suggesting a killer whale quit licking its lips at the sight of an injured seal. So after considerable thumbnail chewing, Joy decided that if the theory were true, it meant that everything in her imagination was just as real as everything that happened out there in the tedious world where she supposedly lived, so long as she was changed by the experience. Which meant in a way that the entire world of E. A. Peugeot, with all its mystery and monsters, was just as real as anything else in her life—or more so, because the stories had in fact changed her forever.

Now, sitting in class, there was even more proof that the theory was true. Because sitting at her desk, oblivious to everything, it was really as if Joy didn't exist at all. Even Winsome Elementary itself was just a figment of her imagination.

It was bliss.

Then the bell rang. The day was over.

Joy for the first time that day felt exhausted and sore, which didn't seem like a good sign for someone who supposedly didn't exist. With every step up the steep stairs of the bus, the scabs on her knees cracked and split.

She sat down beside Byron, who had already taken his seat and was busy staring vacantly into space. But it was not dreaminess, she noticed, still wincing at her stinging knees. His eyes were shadowy and there was something uncommonly grim about the expression on his chalk-colored face.

The bus pulled away.

Then it hit her. What a terrible sister she'd been. That's what she was really hiding from, pretending not to exist. Byron, her dear loyal brother, had only wanted to get some candy and see a few pumpkins. But instead of leaving him with this happy memory, she'd insisted on dragging him against his will into some black swamp within reach of a vicious, man-eating creature. What unbelievable danger she had put him in! What kind of sister would do such a thing to her little brother?

As the bus weaved its way through Darlington, it became clear to her. She didn't really believe this *solipsism* business, that nothing existed outside of herself. Because the real reason she had brought Byron to the bog was so that he could be her witness, and be modified by the same experience. Which would make things all the more real for her.

She felt sick to think of what he had been through. What an awful sister she was! And selfish! She deserved to be punished. Instead, she'd lied her way out of it and when that wasn't possible, pretended to be in a half coma. Meanwhile Byron, her brother and ever-faithful companion, had kept her secret with little more than a frown.

How he had been changed! Utterly and forever by that unholy terror in the dark bowels of the bog. She looked at his pale little hand with an ugly moon-shaped bruise on it. He was only eight years old! Far too young to have had Death clawing at his heels like that.

In the bog Joy had thought there had been nothing to worry about, because according to E. A. Peugeot, it was only clueless meddlers who were mauled and chomped and crushed and throttled.

But wait, wasn't there another type of character who also usually fell victim to a hideous fate? Joy cast her mind back, running through the scores of stories she'd read in the thick old leather-bound book.

The innocent, she thought. Yes. They were the ones truly eaten like peanuts. Why, Dr. Ingram himself had gone through at least ten hapless assistants alone!

Joy remembered Madame Portia. Her heart rolled over and sunk, just like the poor old woman's home had done the other night. It felt wrong, not telling anyone what had happened. But who would have believed it?

No one would have listened to her, she knew. Certainly not her parents! They would just ground her for making up stories to excuse her irresponsible behavior. But that wasn't the only thing worrying her. After last summer's werewolf incident, Mrs. Wells had threatened to take away *The Compleat and Collected Works* should the book continue to be such a bad influence on her. This time, it would be gone, without a doubt. And with creatures from its very pages on the prowl, that would be a disaster!

So, shouldering terrible guilt unlike anything she'd ever experienced, Joy had resolved to leave the poor old widow where she lay, her home now her tomb, condemned to eternal solitude at the bottom of that black pond.

Out of the corner of her eye, Joy noticed Byron muttering something to himself. That wasn't a good sign, she thought. In the stories of *The Compleat and Collected Works*, a character had three possible fates: lucky to be alive, horribly killed, or completely insane. The last outcome was a particular occupational hazard for the inquisitive Dr. Ingram, who often fretted about losing his mind recalling the abominations he'd encountered on preceding pages. Could Byron's experience have pushed him over the edge? Could he end up gibbering away the rest of his life locked up in someplace like Spooking Asylum? Given his already sensitive nature, it seemed like a no-brainer.

The bus was coming up to the bog, Joy realized nervously as she spotted the large muddy patch cleared before it. A number of cars were parked on it today, she saw with surprise, along with a line of bulldozers belching out black smoke.

The Misty Mermaid project. *Those morons*, thought Joy with horror. *They don't know what's in there!*

Just then there was a terrible impact, throwing the children forward in their seats. Everyone screamed as the bus careened off the road, skidding over the shoulder into the woods. Branches tore at the windows like monstrous fingernails until the vehicle finally came to a stop with a thunderous bang.

CHAPTER 17

The afternoon sun was high and bright, causing Phipps to squint as he burned along the road, trying to make up time. His sunglasses lay on the passenger seat, but his left hand was immobilized in the sling and his right was on the steering wheel. It was trembling, he noticed, as he approached the bog.

He hadn't been back since the terrible events of Halloween, when—ears still ringing from Vince's hideous screams—he'd torn through the woods, moving impossibly across acres of unyielding sphagnum and passing through whipping branches like a ghost. He'd felt nothing—no pain or fear or fatigue. Everything had felt like a dream—a bad dream—that was becoming less and less distinct with each step, until finally coming apart on him as he'd slipped into welcome blackness.

At the sound of a car, he'd awoken shivering by the roadside in his wetsuit. He'd quickly rolled out of sight under an overhanging rock as the headlights briefly illuminated a bulging sack beside him. It was a pillowcase, he'd discovered with confusion, full of Halloween treats.

The kids, he'd then remembered, the ones he'd seen leaping from the sinking house.

He'd gotten up, groaning as the pain in his arm returned. Picking up the pillowcase with his good hand, he'd begun walking, keeping to the shadows as he'd headed back to where he and Vince had parked, a little way out of view on a dark shoulder.

The car keys, he'd then realized—he'd surrendered them to Vince. The thought of his bandmate brought on a fresh attack of revulsion and he'd doubled over again, gagging. Steadying himself, he'd tried the passenger side door, which, thanks to Vince's carelessness, was unlocked. He'd then climbed in and rifled through the glove compartment, hoping he'd left a spare key in there, but found nothing but maps and empty wrappers.

Walking hadn't been an option—someone was sure to call the cops at the sight of a man in a wetsuit limping along the dark streets of Darlington. So he'd slid across to the driver's seat and prized open the underside of the steering column. It had been agonizing work. His broken arm ached, mashed up against the door, and his filthy fingernails tore back painfully with the effort.

Finally, a tangle of wires had fallen into his lap.

Hot-wiring—it was an old skill. He'd learned it back in the days when the band had toured the entire country, stealing a new gassed-up van after every gig. But back then he'd had both hands to work with, and they weren't usually trembling from horror and nausea.

Even one-handed, he hadn't lost his touch, it turned out. Within minutes, the car had awoken with a familiar growl.

He'd driven off without headlights, which were disabled

thanks to his sloppy job with the wires. So he'd rolled slowly forward in the dark, stopping by the side a couple of times to let other nighttime traffic pass him. Then, after reaching his building and parking in the lot, he'd slipped quietly in. He crept past the superintendent's apartment with its TV ever blaring within, scattering a handful of Halloween candy as he went. Then he'd snuck around back, climbing the fire escape to his apartment, where he'd forced open the kitchen window and slithered in.

Squealing in pain, he'd peeled off the wetsuit before getting showered and dressed. He'd then got his spare keys and left his apartment again, dragging the kitchen garbage can out to the main stairwell. There he'd booted it, and it had clattered down, throwing coffee grounds and paper towels and take-out containers everywhere. He'd hurried down after as it rolled to a stop outside the superintendent's front door.

"What's going on out here?" a short man with a red face had shouted, exploding moments later from his apartment in a bathrobe. He'd then spotted someone lying in a heap at the bottom of the stairs. "My heavens, are you all right?"

Phipps had rolled over with a not-entirely faked groan.

"You!" the superintendent had thundered. "I've been ringing your door all night and you never answered!"

"I thought you were a trick-or-treater," Phipps had told him, grimacing. "I'd completely forgotten to buy candy again this year and couldn't bear the thought of disappointed little faces. I was hiding in the dark, ashamed."

"Trick-or-treaters?" the superintendent had scoffed.

"This is a child-free complex! What trick-or-treaters?"

"The ones dropping their candy all over the stairs where tenants can slip on them," he'd lied, pointing to the pile at the superintendent's feet. The man had looked down dumbfounded to see he was standing on a quantity of miniature candy bars. "Now, can you help me up?" Phipps had asked, gritting his teeth as he'd weakly offered his left arm.

The superintendent had then begun hoisting him to his feet. Phipps screamed in agony.

"What? What's wrong?"

"My arm!" Phipps had bellowed at the wide-eyed little man.

"But I hardly touched you!"

"You've gone and broken it, you fool, manhandling me!"

"Don't blame me! You must have done it falling down the stairs!"

"TAKE YOUR HANDS OFF OF ME!" Phipps had shrieked. He'd then limped off toward the parking lot.

"The landlords are evicting you for nonpayment!" the purple-faced superintendent had yelled after him. "That's what I was ringing your door to tell you! You are out of this complex, buddy, out! Do you hear me?"

Phipps had managed a smile as he'd unlocked the car. The exchange had gone off perfectly. After all, the best alibi is not the word of a friend, he knew, but the testimony of an enemy. Should anyone come inquiring after Phipps's whereabouts on Halloween, the superintendent would repel them from the premises, listing all the building policies Phipps had violated that night.

At the hospital his arm had been examined by some grinning young doctor.

"Slipped on candy, eh?" the doctor had repeated jovially. "You look a bit old to be going out on Halloween, Mr. . . . ?"

"Phipps," he'd groaned. "Will this take long, Doctor? I'm in quite a bit of pain and completely exhausted, thank you."

"Sorry, I was just trying to lighten the atmosphere before I snap it back together, which is going to hurt like a b—is going to hurt quite a bit, Mr. Tibbs."

"The name is Phipps—Mr. Phipps!"

There had been a sudden crack, like the breaking bough of some rotten old oak.

"You also seem to have a nasty gash on that finger," the doctor had observed as he pried Phipps's fist from the front of his white coat, which was now smudged with blood. "That will need stitches, Mr. Pips. . . ."

Phipps had then headed home, popping painkillers like breath mints as he drove. Pulling into his apartment complex, he'd managed to wedge his car in crookedly beside the superintendent's van as his head began spinning. Arm in a sling, he'd climbed unsteadily up the garbage-strewn stairs to find a note on his door—CLEAN UP YOUR MESS!—which he'd promptly balled up and tossed over his shoulder. He had bigger messes to clean up, he'd thought darkly, fumbling his keys with one hand.

He'd then kicked the door shut behind him and, losing his balance, had fallen face-first onto the carpet. He'd lain there for a moment, craning his neck to gaze at the inviting couch a mere twelve feet away. Then he'd fallen unconscious.

The next day he'd awoken by the front door. His arm was throbbing. Climbing unsteadily to his feet, he'd quickly swallowed a few of the pills the doctor had given him. They landed in his stomach like hot coals. Wincing, he'd then stumbled over to the telephone to call the mayor.

"You're telling me the old woman's vanished, without a trace? Phipps, that's terrific news!" the mayor had shouted over speakerphone as an exercising apparatus whirred loudly in the background. "Well, then, drag that butt of yours down here and get on the blower—I want to get all the local movers and shakers out for a groundbreaking ceremony tomorrow at four. Maybe even get some TV people in on it too."

"At four tomorrow?" Phipps had repeated.

"Darn right! Let's get this thing going—we're already behind schedule as it is."

"I'm afraid I won't be in to work today," Phipps had said, explaining how he'd injured himself falling down some stairs.

"Well, I suppose I can handle it from here," the mayor had replied wearily. "Okay, take the day off, and tomorrow morning while you're at it. Just make sure you're there for the ceremony in the afternoon—I need you to glad-hand the media to make sure we're the top story."

"Yes, sir."

Phipps had put the phone down and collapsed on the leather couch as the powerful painkillers began numbing his system. Nothing could stop the project now. Once completed, the Misty Mermaid Water Park could begin its most important work: the suffocation of Spooking. Tourists and traffic would descend on the area, causing developers to swarm over the hill—buying it up and knocking it down to begin afresh and build anew.

Then the name of Spooking would be gone forever. Oh, perhaps not completely, Phipps imagined. A horror-themed mini-golf course might be erected in its memory, or it might live on as Spooking's, a family restaurant admired as much for its fine views as its french fries. But the name would never again appear as a town on any maps or on anyone's lips.

And then the curse would be broken. Or so Phipps hoped. After all, how could anyone return to a place that no longer existed? Even the bitterest hex couldn't be immune to the forces of irrefutable logic! And what sorcery in history has ever resisted the forward march of progress?

It was a faint hope, Phipps had to admit, but it hardly mattered. No matter what, Spooking would be destroyed. And if he was to be condemned for the deeds of a dead relative, he would have to at least take satisfaction in murdering the man's precious muse.

Exhausted, Phipps had then closed his eyes. But a vision had kept haunting him: an image of Vince thrashing at the center of a sickening red foam. Terrible sounds had echoed in his skull again, an awful cacophony of fear and agony that made him pitch forward on the couch. The horrible truth, lying in wait at the center of the bog—would it be buried when the bulldozers finally blazed through, or simply unearthed? His mind had spun at all the hideous possibilities until he'd fallen unconscious.

It was the next day and already five minutes past four

as Phipps rolled the window back up. He was running late. Braking hard, he signaled to turn off into the muddy lot by the bog. He could already see an impressive turnout of businesspeople milling about as bulldozers stood ominously in the background, belching smoke. A television station van was just unloading, he noted with satisfaction. He felt his nerves calm and his grip on the wheel become confident again as he turned.

Then he saw it, appearing suddenly in his rearview mirror—and bearing down on him like a yellow monster.

The infernal Spooking school bus.

Phipps gunned the engine, the thick tires screeching as he tried to get out of the way. But it was too late. There was a crunch. His head slammed off the steering wheel as the black car was sent flying off the road into the bog.

A flare of pain woke him up. The front of his car was wrapped around a tree stump and white steam hissed up around the crumpled hood. Beyond the cracked windshield, a figure approached at great speed from the depths of the bog itself.

"Are you all right in there?" Phipps heard someone shout as the door was flung open. Turning in a daze, he saw it was a man wearing chest-high fishing waders.

"Huh?" asked Phipps, trying to bring the blurry letters on the man's cap into focus.

"You've been in an accident! Are you all right?"

"Yes," answered Phipps dully. "I need to get to the ceremony. Wait—did someone bring the ribbon and scissors?"

"Please sir, just relax—we'll get you out of there!"

Just then the mayor arrived, having raced across the parking area with a group of men and women in business suits trailing behind like baby ducks. They stopped on the bank just opposite, apparently unsure if the dramatic circumstances merited plunging expensive shoes into the dirty brown creek running under the car.

"Phipps, my man!" yelled the mayor. "Are you okay down there? It looks like you overshot the parking lot, buddy!" The assembled businesspeople stood by awkwardly as the mayor laughed at the terrifying accident as if it were part of the scheduled entertainment.

The television crew caught up and began recording, panning from the chuckling mayor to the yellow school bus full of stunned children to the hissing black car.

"I'm fine," snapped Phipps irritably, coming to his senses. "I just want to get out of here." He began struggling to undo his seat belt with his right hand.

"Hold still," the man in the waders ordered. "I'm trying to help you."

"Leave me alone!"

"Ahoy down there!" called the mayor. "And who exactly might you be? I ask because not only is this private property, but a restricted construction area. And the only thing you're likely to catch in that disgusting swamp is a cold."

"I'm not fishing," replied the man in the waders indignantly. He turned, pointing to the letters on his cap. "I'm Field Agent Wagner from FISPA—the Federal Imperiled Species Protection Agency."

"Ah!" A broad smile suddenly appeared across the

mayor's face. "Ah-ha-ha! Good day to you, sir. I'm Mayor MacBrayne, of Darlington City Council. You've come to check on those wonderful turtles, no doubt. Well, I have good news! My assistant—that's him down there in the car crash—my assistant assures me they have all been happily relocated. Haven't they, Mr. Phipps?" The mayor flashed his teeth at the video camera.

"That's great, but I'm not here about the turtles, mayor," replied Agent Wagner testily. "There has been a development concerning the status of this wetland."

"A development?" asked the mayor, bemused. A few businesspeople began shuffling uncomfortably around him. "What development?"

"I received a curious call at my office last week," Agent Wagner said to the crowd hovering above him. "A very curious call indeed. A person—a child possibly—drew my attention to some correspondence sent to our agency concerning this very bog."

"A child? Sounds like a prank call to me. Kids today!" The mayor chortled. He turned to wave to the little faces pressed up to the windows of the immobilized school bus. "I just usually hang up as soon as they ask if my refrigerator is running."

"I said *possibly*—I'm not entirely sure who it was," continued Agent Wagner. "But it is of little consequence. The point is, the caller brought to my attention a local expert by the name of Dr. Ludwig Zweig. Dr. Zweig had recently forwarded to me his research surrounding a rather incredible discovery. Unfortunately, the package was lost in transit for several weeks, during which time the poor old fellow apparently passed away. However, as it happened, the materials found their way into my inbox just before I received the unusual phone call."

A moan escaped the black car, but no one noticed. They were all hanging on Agent Wagner's every word.

"Upon hearing the name, I promptly opened the package and read with astonishment about an alleged organism living right here in Spooking Bog—a completely new and undiscovered species, so the research claimed. And having been reminded by this mysterious caller about a development project about to get underway here, I decided to come out and investigate right away."

"Well, I'm so sorry you wasted your time, Agent," said the mayor apologetically. "This Zweig character was a well-known eccentric—a kook, if you will. And a bit of a prankster, it seems, much like a child."

"On the contrary, my time was not wasted at all," replied Agent Wagner. "Using the precise GPS coordinates Dr. Zweig provided, I was able to follow this brook straight to where it runs off at the very heart of the bog. And there, growing around some foul sinkhole, I encountered a new species of considerable significance."

"Bravo!" cheered the mayor. "Well then, another adorable creature to relocate. Just point it out and I'll get my best men on it. Because we want to make sure this project gets off on the right foot!"

"That's the problem," answered Wagner. "It's not a creature at all. It's a plant, in fact, of the carnivorous variety.

Commonly known as a pitcher plant—except this particular species is so big that it can swallow up entire frogs and rats whole. I'm talking about a scientific anomaly that only seems to thrive in this specific bog. In my entire career, I've never seen anything quite like it.

"Which also means, I'm afraid, that any construction project is out of the question at the moment. I'm recommending that the bog be reclassified as the habitat of an imperiled species, with all protections and exclusions granted under the law."

The businesspeople began murmuring among themselves.

"But Mr. Wagner, be reasonable," said the mayor. "If it's just a few plants we're talking about, what's the big deal? Surely we can just pot the suckers and put them in a nice warm solarium somewhere."

"I must also warn you that from this moment anyone tampering with this site risks fines of up to one million dollars as well as criminal prosecution."

At this pronouncement, several businesspeople began checking their watches and setting off in the direction of their cars, whistling tunelessly to themselves.

The mayor bared his teeth at Agent Wagner. Then, noticing the video camera pointing at him again, he reshaped his grimace into a stiff grin: "Now, now, Mr. Wagner, there must be some kind of mistake—"

A series of horn blasts from the black wreck interrupted him.

The television camera turned, zooming in on Phipps as he butted his head against the steering wheel. After one final blast, he climbed out of the car, wearing a twisted expression under his horribly swollen brow. After stumbling around for a moment glaring in every direction, he opened his mouth as if to say something—but then hung his head and stood there, the brown brook swirling around his knees as something bobbed up in front of him, looking for all the world like the sickly underbelly of a ragged dead fish.

Except that it had an ace of spades and the words "Live Hard" tattooed on it.

Then someone started screaming.

CHAPTER 18

Joy hurried down to breakfast. She'd hardly slept, jumping up the moment her alarm went off. She quickly threw on her clothes and ran downstairs, where Byron already sat at the table, eating cereal. Her father, she saw, was just unfolding the morning newspaper.

"Does it say anything about the school bus accident in there?" demanded Joy impatiently. "Does it say anything about FISPA?"

"FISPA?" asked Mr. Wells. "Why in the world would it say anything about them?"

"Um, why not?" answered Joy evasively. The truth was, after the accident yesterday, she'd seen a man in a FISPA hat. It was Field Agent Wagner, she was sure of it, come to investigate the bog fiend! And he'd caused quite a commotion, by all appearances. Although she couldn't hear what he was saying from inside the bus, the crowd soon began screaming and shrieking—one person even upchucked!

"Oh dear!" her father exclaimed.

"What is it?" asked Mrs. Wells.

"Horror Show in Spooking Bog," he read aloud.

"What does it say?" cried Joy. "What does it say?"

"Apparently they found a piece of an arm right where you had your accident yesterday!"

Joy's spoon landed in the center of her bowl, sending milk flying everywhere as Byron shot back in his chair, eyes bulging.

Mrs. Wells turned with a glare. "Edward, do you really think you should be reading that out loud to the children?"

"Why, you know how much they love gory stories, Helen."

"Yes, but perhaps not real ones where they were actually at the scene!"

"Oh yes, I suppose you're right," agreed Mr. Wells. "Never mind, children. Go on, eat your cereal."

"Dad!" cried Joy.

"Your breakfast, Joy," said Mrs. Wells sternly.

It was no use arguing. Joy's cereal turned to the consistency of wallpaper glue as she painfully watched her father read the entire story, gasping occasionally at some horrific detail.

"Well, I suppose I'd better head off to work," said Mr. Wells, tucking the folded newspaper behind the toaster on the counter. "I don't know if there'll be any delays at the bottom of the hill, what with the police searching for more body parts and everything."

"Edward!" cried Mrs. Wells from the sink.

"Oh yes, sorry, dear," he said. "Good-bye, everyone. Have a nice day."

"Please finish up, children, or you'll miss your bus," said Mrs. Wells sweetly. "Or if you'd like, I can always drive you today if you're feeling a bit nervous about the bus. . . ."

"We'll take our chances," said Joy crankily, pushing her bowl away.

After brushing their teeth and collecting their school bags, they stood at the front door, waiting. A shiny replacement bus pulled up and the children headed out to meet it.

"Wait!" cried Joy. "I forgot something!"

"Hurry!" Mrs. Wells sounded exasperated as Joy ran back into the house. "Byron, ask the bus driver if he minds waiting just one more minute!"

But before Byron's short legs even made it halfway to the street, Joy had already come flying out the front door after him.

"That was fast," observed Mrs. Wells as her daughter ran down the path with something hidden in her sling. Then she remembered the newspaper behind the toaster. "Joy Wells!" she called out.

"Bye, Mom!" Joy shouted back, leaping onto the moving bus.

⁂ ⁂ ⁂

"THE GHOULS ON THE BUS GO ROUND AND ROUND, ROUND AND ROUND, ROUND AND ROUND . . ."

Oblivious, Joy pushed her way through the laughing throng, digesting what she'd read in the newspaper now safely tucked in the crook of her cast. So that's what all the screaming had been about—they'd found part of someone's arm floating in the creek next to the car the bus had hit. It explained why so many policemen came swooping in shortly after, yelling for someone to get the children out of there. Within minutes, a replacement bus arrived and they were driven away from the chaotic scene.

Joy shuddered at the possibility that the limb belonged to poor Madame Portia, but quickly dismissed the thought. While the old woman might have had some sort of professional interest in cards, Joy couldn't picture her getting an ace of spades tattoo, or picking "Live Hard" as her personal catchphrase. The arm had to have belonged to someone else, she was convinced. The authorities, meanwhile, were sweeping the bog, searching for evidence, the paper said.

On page two, Joy discovered a delightful headline: FISPA PULLS PLUG ON WATER PARK.

So Joy was right—it was Field Agent Wagner she'd spotted in action! With his broad shoulders and strong brow, he'd seemed even more commanding than on the phone—the exception being those ridiculous fishing waders, which were a bit of an unexpected visual. A number of cool-sounding Agent Wagner quotes peppered the article, including one crediting "an anonymous tip" that prompted his investigation.

Still, Joy felt disappointed by his findings. That was it? The amazing secret of Dr. Ludwig Zweig was some big plant that eats rats and frogs? It was kind of interesting, she supposed, with an element of the grotesque, but it just wasn't doing it for her. Something you could lay low with a weed-whacker wasn't quite the unstoppable monster she was expecting.

But wait a second, thought Joy. In "The Bawl of the

Bog Fiend," what had Dr. Ingram noted just before poor Dickson fell down that dark hole to his doom?

"A ring of striking specimens, hooded and monstrous, resembling in all but size a genus deadly to anything seeking the source of its sweet scent."

They weren't poisonous mushrooms—they were pitcher plants! Giant ones, full of sweet nectar to attract their prey. And where had Dr. Ingram uncovered them? At the entrance to the den of the bog fiend!

As far as anyone knew, the article also said, these ancient plants only survived thanks to the unique ecosystem of this particular bog. Which was even more hard evidence that E. A. Peugeot's stories were set around Spooking!

Trembling with excitement, Joy shoved the newspaper into her decrepit old desk.

"So, children, how are we today?"

"GREAT, MISS KEENER!" shouted Joy along with everyone.

CHAPTER 19

Earlier that same morning in a cramped kitchen, a wooden clock ticked noisily against a background of bright sunflower wallpaper.

"What's wrong, Morris?" asked Mrs. Mealey timidly, sitting at the kitchen table. "You look so cross."

Morris threw down the newspaper, his face twisted with disgust. "It's the Misty Mermaid Water Park, Mother!" he cried. "It's ruined, ruined, ruined!"

"What do you mean, dear?"

"FISPA has completely shut us down!" barked Morris, his mother wincing with fright. "They found some sort of idiotic plant in the bog where the park was to be built, and now they've put the entire area under an environmental protection order!" He slammed a fist on the table. "Who cares about a stupid plant? We are talking about the future of Darlington here!"

"What a crying shame!" Mrs. Mealey declared. "Excuse me, sweetheart, but who is FISPA?"

"The Federal Imperiled Species Protection Agency, Mother!" cried Morris. "Honestly, what's the point of subscribing to the newspaper if you don't keep yourself informed?"

"I get it for *you*, of course," cooed Mrs. Mealey. "To nourish your gift. You know I don't like reading it. There's so much awful news in the world, and I just don't want to know about it. If it had been up to me, I would have canceled the silly thing as soon as your father vanished."

"For the twentieth time, Father didn't *vanish*," objected Morris. "He took off on us."

"Stop saying that!" Mrs. Mealey fumbled with her apron strings. "I saw it myself, with my own eyes. But it doesn't matter—your father is coming back someday, I know it. He told me so, in a dream," she said. She stared off, as if into some invisible infinite vastness. "His body was all see-through-ish, and he said he just had a little plumbing job on the other side to finish, then they'd let him return to our world. . . ."

Morris sighed—he was so tired of this. "But who are *they*, Mother?"

"The ones that took him, of course," replied Mrs. Mealey with a nervous laugh. "Now, what were you saying about your water park? Is this something to do with that season pass you won?"

"Mother, to blazes with the season pass!" he exploded. "The whole park is finished!" Seeing his mother now on the verge of tears, Morris took a few deep breaths and managed to calm himself. "And to make matters worse, they pulled somebody's arm out of the bog, so on top of everything else, it's now a crime scene as well."

The color drained from Mrs. Mealey's face.

"Mother, it wasn't Father's arm, unless he had a big tattoo

he didn't tell you about. For heaven's sake. But it's what the city administration would call a public relations nightmare." Morris glanced up. "Would you look at the clock. Aren't you watching the time, Mother? I'm going to be late for school!"

Mrs. Mealey hurriedly assembled a lunch as Morris gave his teeth a quick brush. He flattened his hair with a thick daub of pomade—his father's brand, which his mother kept replenishing—and then with a comb gave his hair a careful side parting.

Morris looked at himself in the mirror, adjusting his clip-on bow tie as his hair began struggling free. He sighed. By the time he arrived at school, sputtering and coughing after a three-block run, the part in his hair would be obliterated, as usual.

❧ ❧ ❧

Byron felt much better. The routine of school, including the habitual abuse, had acted like a kind of Band-Aid over the psychic injuries inflicted on Halloween. He felt like himself again, sitting in the flickering fluorescent light of his class, staring at the strawberry-blond drapery Lucy Primrose tucked casually behind her ear.

Morris arrived late and out of breath, carrying his foul mood like a frayed flag into battle. Byron found himself snickering inwardly as from the depths of Mrs. Whipple's purse came a muffled electronic version of Beethoven's "Ode to Joy."

"Morris, you're here! This is an important call," the teacher said, hustling out of the classroom. "Please watch the class for five minutes."

Morris dumped his books on his desk and stomped up to the front of the class. "Read quietly!" he barked at them. His head then landed on Mrs. Whipple's desk with a painful-sounding thump.

Byron chuckled to himself, then turned to gaze at his princess again. He was startled to see that she was looking straight at him, laughing as well. A bolt of terror pierced his heart. What should he do? Then some unknown force formed an *L* out of his thumb and forefinger and coolly raised it to his forehead, which made Lucy giggle.

"I SAID QUIETLY!" shouted Morris.

And Byron's spirits soared, like a thousand starlings pin-wheeling into an ink blue sky while roman candles exploded above.

❧ ❧ ❧

"So the answer is? Anyone?"

It was late in the day. Joy sat in Miss Keener's classroom, yawning as she drew on her cast with a marker. Her plan was to fill in the blank areas with tiny little skulls, but she had a lot of real estate left to cover, seeing as no one was exactly lining up to sign it.

"Joy?"

Nuts—it was even more proof she did still exist.

"I don't know, Miss Keener," shrugged Joy.

Miss Keener scrunched up the corner of her mouth. "Louden?"

"I don't know either, Miss Keener," Louden answered lamely.

Joy looked over at him.

With everything that had happened in the bog, she had forgotten all about her awkward experience stuck in the laundry room with Louden. She cringed to remember scuttling away like some disgusting beetle whose patio-slab apartment had been unexpectedly upturned. Another face-to-face with the bog fiend sounded more appealing than feeling that way again.

"What is it with this class today?" said Miss Keener. "Did you all eat junk food for lunch or something?"

Louden hadn't spoken to Joy since Halloween or even turned an eye, black or otherwise, in her direction. That was fine, as far as she was concerned. But then she caught herself suddenly thinking about his tight-fitting skeleton costume, and how he'd reminded her of a lean young racehorse—skinny-limbed and a bit awkward, but already beginning to show the powerful frame that would one day thunder across finish lines.

Blushing at the thought, she turned away, blaming the odd fluttery feeling in her stomach on the hastily swallowed sandwich she'd eaten while leafing through the newspaper again. Her mother was always on her case about chewing her food properly—maybe her mom was right.

Joy put down the marker, bored with drawing skulls. Instead, she slipped a protractor from her desk and began to sneakily gouge the surface of her desk, outlining a small heart on the last unmarked area available.

JW, she carefully scratched inside of it.

"Anyone know?" asked Miss Keener.

She drew a plus sign.

"Come on, class, this is going to be on the test . . . Cassandra?"

Joy finished, then blew the sawdust away from the carved initials. EAP—Ethan Alvin Peugeot. Forever. The bell rang, and she stood up with a quiet sigh of relief.

The class began filing out noisily as Joy pushed her chair in. She bent over to search the dark, disorganized interior of her desk compartment for the newspaper, which she thought best to slip back behind the toaster when she got home.

As she stood up, something caught her eye, jammed in the inkwell. She stared suspiciously at the orange shape before curiosity got the better of her, and she stuffed her hand into the sharp-sided hole. Awkwardly, she drew the object out, pinched between her fingertips. It was a little paper bag with a black cat on it, she saw with surprise, filled with candy.

Happy Halloween, it said.

Joy felt a jolt. Looking up, she caught Louden slinking out of the classroom.

Her face bright red, she slipped the bag into her pocket, then began checking and rechecking the various notebooks she'd packed for homework.

"Joy, you'll miss your bus home if you don't go now," warned Miss Keener finally.

Joy hurried out. Outside, she joined Byron in the line. It was the old Spooking bus this time, its front bumper now hammered roughly back into shape, and coughing out the same familiar blue cloud of fumes. The door remained shut while the driver finished eating a burrito.

Morris M. Mealey drew up to them. "Byron, you fat-headed lunk," he snapped. "Do you mind clearing the sidewalk? This is a pedestrian throughway, you know!"

Byron began raising the *L*, but his sister jumped in first.

"Don't talk to my brother that way, you mop-headed little jerk," she said rather merrily.

"Oh, it's the gruesome-twosome—I'm so frightened!" mocked Morris. "Out of my way, Spooking freaks, before I report you to Principal Crawley for deliberately impeding my progress." With a pair of sharp little elbows, he then shoved his way through.

"Hey, Morris," called Joy after him. "Did you hear? It looks like I won that contest of yours after all."

Morris whirled like some feral creature whose tail had been set on fire. "What?"

"The Darlington, City of the Future contest," she repeated. "It looks like they picked my idea over yours in the end, even though I just phoned in my entry a couple of days ago. But I guess they liked it so much that they didn't care it was late."

"What are you talking about? What *idea*?"

"You know," said Joy. "The one about making Spooking Bog the protected home of an imperiled species, instead of building some idiotic water park full of lame mermaids. Pretty good plan, huh?" The bus door suddenly folded open with a bang and Joy gently prodded Byron forward onto the bus. "Anyway," called Joy, "I'm sure you could trade your season passes for a nice FISPA baseball cap or something."

The door folded shut behind them. Morris stood quivering

with rage on the sidewalk as Joy gave him a cheery little wave from above.

Morris glared at the bus as it pulled away, wishing with all his heart for some sort of supernatural power to will gas tanks into exploding.

Just then, a hand seized the back of his jacket as someone growled: "Mealey."

Morris squeaked. "Mr. Phipps!" he burst out. But his relief was fleeting—there was something about the man's face that Morris found incredibly frightening. "What happened to your arm?" he squeaked, noticing the sling.

"Some idiot dropped a house on it. But let's not talk about that. Let's take a walk instead."

"Sure," answered Morris timidly. "Is there anything I can help you with?"

Phipps slapped his hand heavily on the boy's shoulder as they began walking away from the school.

"You can help me get to the bottom of something," replied Phipps, flashing an amiable smile at the crossing guard.

"Anything for the mayor, of course," said Morris. "Except I don't live in this direction."

"No?" said Phipps. "Pity."

CHAPTER 20

Phipps ushered the trembling boy along. The truth was, he took no pleasure in menacing children, but then again, he wasn't sure this kid quite counted. Mealey seemed more like a groveling little goblin, really, than a defenseless child.

And with that in mind, Phipps felt a bit less monstrous.

Not that he had much capacity for sympathy anymore. The world was a cruel place after all. Sometimes bad things happened and you just had to accept that. And if bad things had to be done sometimes, you had to accept that too.

Morris looked up fearfully at the man in black hovering above him like a vulture with a beady eye locked on some legless little animal. They had been walking in silence for some time. Glancing over his shoulder, Morris saw Winsome Elementary slip from view entirely.

"Are we almost there?" croaked Morris finally. "My mother will be getting worried. She waits for me to get home so she can find out what I want for dinner. And I always head straight home."

They drew up to the edge of a golf course, leaf-strewn

and deserted, the fairways now sodden and brown.

"This is far enough," said Phipps, stopping. It was time to put an end to this exercise—too late, he knew, but it was the principle of the thing. He could not tolerate meddlers, no matter how toadlike or seemingly insignificant. Just look at the results! The blueprints of his visionary plan for Darlington—and Spooking—were no more than smoking ash, thanks to a couple of elementary school children. The ones he'd seen in the bog, including a tubby little dark-haired boy.

"Do you golf, Mr. Mealey?"

"Er, no sir."

"That's a shame. All young politicos should golf, you know." Phipps took an awkward but nevertheless vicious one-handed swing as Morris cringed. "Darlington has some very nice courses, thanks to our own beloved Mayor MacBrayne. He was a big figure in the golf industry before moving into politics. Did you know that?"

"No."

"See? You learn something new every day. But I dare say this course here is a bit challenging for a novice. Lots of rough. And the bunkers! Like quicksand! They'd swallow up someone your size—you'd sink right to the bottom and never be found again!"

Morris blinked rapidly, the tight knot of his tie like a plum caught in his throat.

Phipps continued: "Anyway, I have a couple of questions about your letter to my office. Oh, and thanks, by the way, for your kind offer to assist the re-election campaign for

Mayor MacBrayne. Fortunately, the Mayor still has another two years left in his term of office."

"Oh," replied Morris. "That's great."

"Yes. But the sentiment was appreciated. Now back to your letter, wherein you mentioned something about the site of the upcoming Misty Mermaid Water Park."

"Yes! I so agreed that Spooking Bog is the perfect place for it! I mean, was, anyway . . ."

Phipps ground his teeth. "Actually it was the only place for it, as we learned from our surveys of the area," he replied. "In fact, nowhere else around Darlington could accommodate such a development, which means there can be no Misty Mermaid ever now."

"What a crying shame," said Morris, blushing to think how much like his mother he sounded.

"Yes, it is," agreed Phipps. "But what's done is done. What I'm much more interested in is who did what, and when. You see, I found it a bit odd that you knew all about our plans for Spooking Bog, since we hadn't even made them public yet."

"Really?"

"Really. That way no tree-hugging hippies could overreact to a few minor items and shut our project down. But thanks to some unknown person, it became very public, very quickly— thanks to someone who not only wrote to us about our secret plans for Spooking Bog, but then called the Federal Imperiled Species Protection Agency, I hear . . ."

"It wasn't me, I swear!" cried Morris. "I didn't tell anyone!"

"Then who did?" demanded Phipps fiercely. "How did

you know about it in the first place? Don't lie to me, Mealey, or we'll be having a closer look at the sand trap over there."

"Lucy Primrose's birthday party!" burst out Morris, drawing a blank look from Phipps. "Remember? You were dressed like a fool."

"I was a wandering minstrel!" roared Phipps. "Do you hear me?"

"The blond-haired girl I was talking to," wailed Morris. "Joy Wells—the Spooky. She was the one who told me, honest!" Morris broke into a series of heaving sobs. "She even laughed right in my face about it, about stopping the Misty Mermaid, just now as she was getting on the bus before you grabbed me. Please, Mr. Phipps, you've got to believe me. I would never do anything to hurt your administration. Ever!"

Phipps looked down at the pitiful little boy, eyes bright with tears. He was loathsome—a pathetic little toady like none other. But at least he was playing for the right side. That should count for something.

The Spooking girl. She'd reminded him of himself, he remembered—a born outcast living in a childlike dream, looking down her nose at the world as it went on turning without her. He remembered her defiant eyes flashing as he tried to forewarn her of the coming sting of disillusionment. He had hoped to save her some pain.

This was her thanks.

"Morris," said Phipps in a soothing voice. "I'm sorry if I made you cry. You see, sometimes grown-ups get very upset when things that were going so right go suddenly so wrong.

And that's why it's important to always tell them the truth, which I'm glad you did."

Morris nodded, sniffing violently.

"The Misty Mermaid was a great idea—your idea—and I'm very upset that our fellow Darlingtonians will never get to enjoy it," said Phipps. "But don't worry. We'll think of more great ideas, you and I, hmm? Now, let me walk you home," he finished, trying to wipe away the waxy film left on his hand after ruffling the boy's hair.

"Okay," answered Morris, dabbing his nose with the sleeve of his blazer.

"Hey, would you like to meet the mayor, Morris? I would be happy to arrange it. He even has some fun stuff in his office you might enjoy, like video games, a ping-pong table . . ."

"I don't play sports," answered Morris flatly. "Or with toys."

"Of course not. My apologies."

"But I would still like to meet the mayor," he quickly added.

"Consider it done," assured Phipps. "And bring your mother and father if you'd like."

"That would be a good trick," Morris told him. "My father disappeared over a year ago—or vanished into thin air if you believe my mother. No, I'll be coming alone, thanks."

Phipps felt a prickling sensation crawl up his back as his eyes darted to the plump little face bobbing along beside him.

CHAPTER 21

There was a stirring within the folds of Joy's coat as she made her way along the frigid streets of Spooking. Poor Fizz, she thought—how awful of her to have plucked him from under his heating lamp to suffer this icy gale. He was stuffed into a canvas bag Joy had hung from her cast, lined with one of Melody Huxley's fox stoles which, though once pretty swanky, looked an awful lot like a mangy old piece of roadkill. The stole was working some sort of magic, however—stroking Fizz back to sleep, it felt positively toasty in there.

Byron had passed on Joy's invitation to go for a walk. She'd found him on the stairs, playing with the new knight figures he'd bought with his allowance money.

"No thanks," he'd answered formally without looking up.

"How come?" asked Joy, surprised. Byron always came along when she asked.

"I just don't feel like going outside," he'd said, shrugging. "It looks cold out there."

"All right." Joy had hovered as Byron returned to his figures, making the sounds of steel clashing against steel. A black knight soon fell howling off a carpeted cliff. "Are you mad at me or something?" she asked.

"Nope. I'm busy playing."

"Okay," Joy had said. She had turned to go before noticing something. "Is that one of my old princess figurines tied to the stair rail?"

"I'm in the middle of a game!" Byron had thundered at her. "Do you mind?"

"Sorry," she'd cried, scuttling off.

So she'd settled for a snoozy Fizz instead. From deep within the bag under her overcoat, she could make out his snores over the howling wind.

A pair of wintering crows shivered atop the stone wall as Joy slipped into the cemetery. She was thinking about the letter she'd received yesterday.

Dear Miss Wells,

Thank you very much for your correspondence. I so enjoyed reading about Spooking, which sounds delightfully atmospheric. A perfect place, I am sure, for sitting back with a warm cup of cocoa and reading a few eerie tales.

Regarding your suggestion that Spooking was both the home and inspiration of Mr. Peugeot, I can only say that while that is a nice thought, literary scholars are in agreement that the author most likely lived to the north, somewhere in the vicinity of Holetown. Perhaps you might convince your parents to take you on a trip there someday! I am sure you will find it is as intriguing as I did during my many visits.

It was very nice to hear from you. Keep the strange fires of
EAP burning!

Sincerely,
Richard Strang
President and Treasurer, EAP Society

P.S. Please find our winter newsletter enclosed.

Joy had wrinkled her nose in disgust. Holetown? Who
would even stop off for lunch somewhere with a name like
that, much less bang out a thousand pages about it? No,
these supposed literary scholars were obviously quite inca-
pable of reading between the lines. Peugeot lived in Spooking. Joy was certain.

She had read the letter over a few times, blushing whenever she came to the bit about her parents taking her on a
trip. It was all a bit assuming really, considering she'd never
even mentioned her age. Was it her stationery? Joy cringed
to picture the floral sheets with their happy little ladybugs
that her mother had helpfully provided.

But surely the sharp-minded souls at the EAP Society
were interested in more than just stationery. Thinking it
over, she was actually impressed that they weren't easily
swayed. These were clever people after all, ever on guard
against pretenders and charlatans. Clearly she just hadn't
made the case for Spooking strongly enough. She needed
better evidence, something that would prove the author's
residence beyond a shadow of a doubt.

Joy had then unfolded the newsletter, which was stapled together a bit straighter this time. She'd flicked through the pages absently.

Then a photo had caught her eye. An old picture of a stocky man with a square jaw and ruddy face, wearing a brimmed hat tilted roguishly to one side. He was grinning affably as a crowd pushed in on him. A caption read:

Private Investigator "Snake" Buckner, signing autographs after bringing notorious bank robber Mad Dog McBlain to justice. This photograph was taken only a month before his disappearance while pursuing the whereabouts of Ethan Alvin Peugeot.

Joy had yanked open her desk drawer. Taking out the black pen Madame Portia had given her, she'd examined the image of Buckner scribbling on a piece of outstretched paper. His pen was identical! The same shiny black with a snake curling around the cap—it was clear even in the old grainy photograph. But how could it have ended up at the bottom of that pond?

Joy had recalled Madame Portia telling her how her husband had found all sorts of things down there that the bog had swallowed up, even an old railway station. A railway station! Wasn't that where the private investigator—this Buckner guy—had last sent a telegram to Peugeot's publisher just before he vanished?

It made total sense—the bog fiend had probably snatched Buckner right off the platform and dragged him into the swamp! The pen was proof, Joy had realized, if not of the bog fiend then at least of where the private investigator had disappeared just after locating Peugeot. Joy had punched her pillow in frustration—if only she'd known about it before she'd sent her letter off!

Now, standing among the old headstones, Joy imagined poor Snake Buckner's dreadful resting place—dank and disgusting, his bones now mingling with what was left of the bog fiend's latest victim. The grim image made her puzzle again over whose arm they'd found there, floating in the brook by the road. Was it some foolish meddler or another innocent victim like Buckner? The person's identity, however, was still a mystery. Amid much unprecedented panic around Darlington, the police had been unable to determine the limb's owner other than to confirm it as the upper arm of an adult Caucasian male. No missing persons were reported, however, and a difficult but thorough search failed to turn up any more evidence. It was as if the bog had gobbled up all traces of whatever frightful story had played out in there, according to a particularly dramatic TV news report. Even a murder weapon hadn't been determined, with forensic investigators reporting that the remains were "contaminated by animal activity."

It was looking more and more like the authorities would never find out what really happened in there. Which was for the best in Joy's opinion. Just like in the many tales of E. A. Peugeot, sometimes it was better to end on a question mark. Otherwise, what would be the final chapter? The bog fiend would never put up its claws and come quietly, she knew—blood and guts would fly big-time. And then, never to be outdone when it came to graphic displays of violence, humanity would respond in kind: by pulling out enough firepower to make even an Ultradroid wet itself.

The rare and precious ecosystem in the wondrous Spooking Bog would soon be reduced to a smoldering heap, Joy had no doubt.

It was with this in mind that Joy had nervously chewed her nails, hair, and even the seat in front of her every morning as the bus careened down the road from Spooking Hill. Each time, she'd gasped to see another cluster of vehicles parked by the bog—belonging to police, FISPA agents, and legions of experts come to study Ludwig's awe-inspiring plants. In other words, a variety pack of human chew-toys, Joy had thought. But by each afternoon the vehicles were gone, their passengers evidently unmolested. How could that be? In "The Bawl of the Bog Fiend," the creature's attacks only stopped once the villagers began staying well away. Could it be injured? Asleep? Or could the bog fiend, with the shred of diabolical intelligence attributed to it by Peugeot, actually recognize those bringing balance rather than destruction to its habitat? Whatever the reason, the activity around its foul den was certainly being ignored.

Meanwhile, the citizens of Darlington were settling back down in their nauseating dens as well, Joy had noticed. Soon the mystery surrounding whatever grisly events had transpired within the bog's mucky interior would be forgotten, along with any amazing carnivorous specimens that might lurk inside. The macabre discoveries would just become part of the many dreadful impressions that kept Darlings away from Spooking Hill, which as far as Joy was concerned was as happy an ending as ever written.

It was at this thought that the wind suddenly dropped. A

strange stillness came over the cemetery. Joy was suddenly surprised to see someone, not far off, bundled up in a new-looking coat and hat. The person squatted by something Joy had never seen in all the time she'd been visiting the cemetery—a newly cut gravestone. Curious, Joy snuck over for a closer look. A pair of hands with long, painted fingernails were visible, delicately arranging what appeared to be sprigs of sphagnum moss. Joy squinted, trying to make out the inscription on the polished stone.

CHERISHED HUSBAND.

Fizz let out an enormous snotty snore. The figure whirled around, a sprig of moss still clenched between her fingers.

"Madame Portia?" cried Joy. She stepped back uncertainly, feeling as if in a dream.

"Oh, hello, my dear!" replied the old woman with delight. "Was that your froggy making that disgusting noise? I hope so, otherwise I think you are in need of some serious antibiotics."

Madame Portia looked radiantly beautiful. Her hair was a brilliant silver and her teeth gleamed like pearls.

"Are you . . . ," began Joy, unsure of her own eyes.

"Alive? Yes, of course! Oh, and I must apologize. It occurred to me that you might have thought I was drowned like a rat, but since I didn't know your address, I was hoping to run into you. And now I have."

Joy breathed a sigh of relief. Despite her best efforts, she had never actually come face-to-face with an actual ghost, and wasn't quite mentally prepared for it at the moment.

"Child!" shrieked Madame Portia. "Your arm!"

Joy looked at her empty coat sleeve. "Oh—it's fine. It's just in a cast, see? I'm getting it taken off tomorrow, actually."

"Goodness gracious. No doubt broken during that horrible calamity on Halloween," said Madame Portia with a shudder. "What an awful memory, that night—never have I been more terrified in all my long life!"

Even with her significantly shorter existence, Joy had to agree. "How did you get out of there?" she asked. "Byron and I just barely made it out."

"It was quite an amazing feat," answered Madame Portia proudly. "After I heard you escape up the ladder—and thank heavens you did—I was quite certain I was done for. Everything was black and the water was rushing in so fast. But then I remembered how I had just finished photographing my husband's scuba gear in the bedroom, in the hopes of getting a better price for it online."

Madame Portia explained how she'd managed to get the respirator working just as the room filled completely with bog water. She'd then floated around in the cold inky water until the horrible squealing noises above finally subsided, after which she'd squeezed out through a porthole to safety.

"So what now?" asked Joy. "Where are you going to live?"

"That's the terrific news!" exclaimed Madame Portia. "As you might expect, I've had enough of bog life now. As romantic as it might have been with my husband, I'm a people person, I've learned, not a rat-catching hermit lady.

"To tell you the truth, Ludwig and I always knew our time together was short, thanks to the abruptly ending life lines on those big hands of his. And Ludwig, bless his heart, insisted on taking out a hefty life insurance policy so that everything would be taken care of once he was gone. At first I thought it was a bit cheap, of course, getting rich off my clairvoyance like that, but my husband convinced me I could always do some good with the money and eventually I relented.

"So after cashing in his policy, I started thinking. What good could an old fortune-teller like me possibly do at this stage of her life? Then I thought about all the other seniors not as fortunate as I—extraordinary people with amazing histories, wasting away in those depressing, overheated rest homes you see down in Darlington. Shouldn't they have somewhere better to go, I thought, somewhere they could be with others like themselves? A lovely old place with proper grounds, and a bit of gypsy flair, perhaps.

"That night it came to me in a dream. A vision of a beautiful old mansion with a fountain out front, tall hedge-rows, and a gorgeous garden overflowing with flowers. On its gates were the words 'The Happy Fates Retirement Estate' in ghostly glowing letters. I woke up and knew that's what I had to do—open a rest home for eccentric old folks like me!

"The next day I found it—the very property I dreamed of—for sale right here in Spooking. So I bought it imme-diately, and plan to open within the month, once the paint-ing and plastering is done. Oh, you and your family will have to come to the grand opening, my dear! You can't miss the place—it's just across from the park beside Spooking Asylum. Oh, I know, perhaps not the perfect spot with all the stories about that sinister old facility, but unfortunately you can't argue with visions! Besides, I've hired a groundskeeper—Hamilton, the young grave-digger who buried Ludwig. I'll just get him to make sure there are no gaps in the barbed wire and I'm sure everything will be fine. Who knows if they even admit dangerous patients anymore, much less let them escape."

Joy had never seen behind the walls of the sprawling mental institution, a setting she recognized from various terrifying tales in *The Compleat and Collected Works of E. A. Peugeot.* Now she'd heard enough—sneaking onto the grounds was definitely going to the top of her to-do list.

"Speaking of your husband," said Joy, changing the subject, "did you hear all the news about his discovery?"

"I most certainly did," replied Madame Portia, beaming. "Our beloved bog is finally safe from that gang of greedy *idiotas.* What wonderful news! And not only that, that handsome man from FISPA informs me that the scientific community has decided to name the plant in honor of my dear Ludwig: *Sarracenia zweig!*"

"That's awesome!" cried Joy. "If only he knew, he would be so proud," she added sympathetically.

"Oh, don't worry about that, dear—I'm going to host a séance soon and let him know all about it. I just first need to sign up a few residents to make a workable spirit circle. But all in due time. Anyway, enough about me—how is young Byron doing? Still as heroic as ever?"

"He's all right, I guess," reported Joy. "He seems a bit weird lately, kind of like he doesn't want much to do with me anymore."

"Miss Joy, I'm sure that isn't true," said Madame Portia gently. "He's just getting older, that's all. I'm certain the little bear knows he's lucky to have a sister like you."

"I don't know about that," replied Joy. "I'm the kind of sister who nearly got her brother killed, remember."

"Nonsense!" exclaimed Madame Portia. "All boys love adventure, but precious few have a sister who would ever take them on such an exciting one. Usually the most a little brother can expect is to be forced into a frilly dress and covered in lipstick. Now you go and ask Byron which he would prefer—a near-death experience or being dressed up like a little dolly. Then you will see exactly how thankful he is."

"Actually, I did once make him wear eye shadow," Joy admitted, "and a tweed skirt."

Madame Portia laughed until it looked like she might fall over. "Spooking is lucky to have a daughter like you," she said, wiping away the tears streaming down her face. "You children are the future of towns such as these. Don't forget it. But excuse me—I must hurry back. Hamilton is moving his things up today and I need to unlock the gatehouse for him."

"It was great to see you again," said Joy, still blushing from her kind words.

"I'll see you soon, I'm sure. Good-bye for now!" called the old fortune-teller as she hurried off.

Alone again, Joy decided to stroll around the cemetery for a while longer. She read the pitted gravestones, each one a familiar old friend. Then the heavy sky cracked above her. Huge wet snowflakes began falling like broken bits of cloud. She stood catching them with her tongue, blinking as they clung to her eyelashes.

Joy squeezed through the rusted cemetery gates and headed along the road back into town. To the right, she could see Darlington stretching out in a neat grid, strangely sunlit and gleaming below. Up ahead, snow continued to whirl around Spooking's steep tangle of avenues, sticking to the hulking houses and ancient trees. Joy stopped, sighing at the beauty of its sudden transformation into stark black and white.

Spooking wasn't dying, thought Joy, whatever that horrible Mr. Phipps said.

Joy had seen him again, stumbling out of his car just after the accident. He'd turned toward her for a moment, glaring at the school bus murderously as she shrunk in her seat. Joy then watched as he flapped in front of a television camera like some tormented crow. There was something familiar in those fierce eyes and lost-in-time features, she was convinced of it.

Whoever he was, he knew nothing about Spooking. Children were its future, just like Madame Portia had said. And people weren't leaving, they were actually coming back! Soon a few dark windows would once again be lit. Spooking did still exist, Joy declared to herself as she walked its streets, and everywhere else could just be a figment of the imagination for all it mattered.

That wasn't exactly true. Spooking was surrounded, Joy knew, and under siege from very real enemies, she now realized.

An army of Darlings sat camped at the foot of the hill, planning their next attack. And no doubt they'd soon come up with some other scheme to make the town into their plaything.

Well, it wasn't going to happen, she decided. Spooking was the inspiration of the famous Ethan Alvin Peugeot! There was no way it could be reduced to some plastic attraction. Someone would have to stop them—a resident expert of the fearless adventuring type.

But who?

"Ah—Miss Joy Wells."

Joy turned with a start. She had just drawn up to the old music shop, a little two-story building standing on a wind-blasted lot, abandoned for as long as she could remember. She hadn't noticed the black car with the smashed-in front and cracked windshield now sitting outside.

It was Mr. Phipps.

"Sorry for scaring you," he said, standing in the doorway of the shop, his arm in a black sling. "I was just trying to be neighborly, seeing as how we're going to be living so close to each other now."

Joy stood speechless for a moment, unable to move as she stared back at the man lurking half in shadow. "You're actually moving up here?" she finally asked incredulously. "To Spooking?"

Phipps cocked an eyebrow, looking for a self-satisfied little smirk on the girl's face. Finding no sign of one, he answered evenly: "Unfortunately, I've found myself between apartments, and since I still have the keys to this old place, I thought I would make myself at home for a little while."

Phipps nodded to the snow-covered boxes jammed in the open trunk. "I would ask for some help with my things, but I see you're missing an arm as well."

"It's broken," Joy replied.

"Painful, I know," said Phipps, wriggling the fingers at the end of his own cast. "How did you hurt yours? In gym class? Falling down stairs, maybe? Or in some sort of bizarre Halloween accident, perhaps?"

"How did you know my last name?" demanded Joy.

"Oh, I beg your pardon—I suppose we haven't been properly introduced. My name is Mr. Phipps. Octavio Phipps. I'm with the mayor's office as I might have mentioned." He held out his hand for a moment before drawing it back unshaken. "How did I know your name? Your friend Morris Mealey mentioned it, I should think."

Joy made a face. "That weird little twerp isn't my friend," she told him sharply.

"My mistake, then," replied Phipps. "I suppose that does make sense—he didn't seem overly fond of you when I spoke with him last. He came right out and blamed you, in fact."

"Blamed me?" exclaimed Joy angrily. "For what?"

"For the Misty Mermaid debacle, of course," answered Phipps. "Wherein the biggest leisure project in the city's history was summarily scuttled just to save some bulbous bit of vegetable matter. Morris said it was you who let FISPA know about the loathsome growths, just to ruin the whole thing."

Joy felt a throb of fear. There was something in Phipps's searching eyes that made her feel like she was standing at the edge of a black pit. "I don't know what he's talking about," she responded with a shrug.

"Well, that's good to hear. I'd thought young Morris was probably mistaken—the boy does seem wound up a bit too tight. And you seem too smart a girl to have done something so silly—something pointless and destructive that only hurts everyone up in Spooking."

"Spooking?" Joy blurted out. "How does losing that dumb water park hurt anybody up here?"

"How does it hurt anybody?" repeated Phipps with a note of comedic offense. "Surely you haven't forgotten our chat about legacies already? Our discussion about the future of Spooking?" He stared at Joy, then shook his head sadly. "Just look here, at this particular legacy," he said, gesturing to the tired-looking building behind him. "A broken-down shop full of expensive old instruments no one plays anymore. The whole thing is worthless now—it just sits here, waiting to collapse. And with no value, it has no future, as I tried to explain to you—no future, like everything else up here.

"But that dumb water park, as you call it, could have changed all that," Phipps continued, his voice rising. "It could have brought people and business and investment like never before. And then this sad decrepit little hill—this legacy of ours—could have finally been worth something!"

"Spooking already *is* worth something," Joy shot back at him. "And it does have a future, because people are moving back."

Phipps beheld the scrappy little girl standing defiantly

before him as her ridiculously old-fashioned coat pooled around her ankles. "Well, I suppose I can't argue your point while unloading my belongings," he said, chuckling. "But it will take a lot more to save this town, you know."

At that moment, Fizz began clawing his way to the top of his bag and growling in his most menacing fashion.

"There's a lovely innocence about you, actually," Phipps continued. He then noticed snarling Fizz poking his head through the buttons of Joy's coat. "And look, you even have a pet frog that thinks it's a dog—how things truly never change around here. And how I would love to tell you not to change—to always stay the same way and never grow up. But that's not possible. No one ever stays the same their whole life. No one stays innocent forever."

Joy kept on her guard as the man gazed off toward the cemetery, its gray outline barely visible in the blowing snow. She held her breath as he suddenly whirled on her, his eyes narrowed to evil-looking slits.

"Which is just as well," he continued. "Because the trouble with the innocent is that they're easily made into victims, you see. And if you're familiar with your scary old stories, you'll know that it's always healthier to be the monster than the victim."

At those words, Phipps suddenly lurched forward. Joy recoiled, desperately holding Fizz back as his toothless jaws snapped viciously at the air. With a casual air, Phipps snatched up a snow-dusted suitcase by her feet.

"See you around Spooking, Joy Wells," he said, stepping back into the doorway. Then he vanished—as if he'd suddenly dissolved into the black interior of the shop. The heavy door closed with an evil creak.

For a moment Joy stood there, rigid with fear in front of the paint-flecked shop. She then crammed Fizz back down into his bag and ran off, hearing him still snarling behind her buttons. The wind began howling, the driving snow blinding Joy as she stumbled past the avenues of Gravesend, Weredale, and Bellevue. Teeth chattering, she finally turned onto Ravenwood. She tore up the path to Number 9, fumbling for the keys in the depths of her coat pockets.

Joy flung the front door open, tripping over something as she leaped inside. It was a pillowcase, mud-streaked and full of candy—with a handwritten note pinned to its side.

Happy Halloween, it said.